Trail To Yesterday

By
Duane Boehm

Trail To Yesterday

Copyright 2019 Duane Boehm

All rights reserved.

For more information or permission contact:
boehmduane@gmail.com

ISBN: 1-676-36452-8

Other Books by Duane Boehm

In Just One Moment
Gideon Johann: A Gideon Johann Western Prequel
Last Stand: A Gideon Johann Western Book 1
Last Chance: A Gideon Johann Western Book 2
Last Hope: A Gideon Johann Western Book 3
Last Ride: A Gideon Johann Western Book 4
Last Breath: A Gideon Johann Western Book 5
Last Journey: A Gideon Johann Western Book 6
Last Atonement: A Gideon Johann Western Book 7
Wayward Brother: A Gideon Johann Western Book 8
Where The Wild Horses Run: Wild Horse Westerns Book 1
Spirit Of The Wild Horse: Wild Horse Westerns Book 2
Wild Horse On The Run: Wild Horse Westerns Book 3
What It All Comes Down To
Hand Of Fate
Wanted: A Collection of Western Stories (7 authors)
Wanted II: A Collection of Western Stories (7 authors)

Dedicated to Willie DuBray

Chapter 1

Bozeman, Montana Territory

For the briefest of moments, as Ike Gunther stood at the well and reeled up the bucket of water, he thought someone had chucked him in the chest with a rock. A tick of a clock later, the roar of the rifle reached his ears. He looked down and saw the blood spurting from the wound. Before he could react, a second shot found its mark. Ike's knees buckled, and as he fell, he whacked his head on the stone wall surrounding the well, rendering him unconscious and near death.

Ike's four ranch hands scurried out of the bunkhouse into the early morning light in various stages of dress while brandishing their guns. They were met with a barrage of gunfire from the two men concealed in the tree line that faced the ranch. The first two men out the door fell from mortal wounds before they ever knew where the shooters hid. Samson Cohen made a dash for the well. His one hand kept his pants hitched up, and in the other, he carried his rifle. In his struggle to run, he lost his grip on his trousers and they fell down, tripping him. Samson made a valiant effort to get to his feet, but a bullet slammed into his temple and he died a humiliating death with his pants bunched up at his ankles. Trace Carson, the lone surviving cowboy, made it to the well and fired the first shot in defense of the ranch.

As Trace returned fire with the attackers, Irene Gunther ran out onto the porch of her ranch home, screaming hysterically.

"What's happening? Is that Ike?" she screamed.

"Get back inside the house. Take the children and go to a bedroom," Trace hollered.

"Is that Ike?" Irene asked again. In her heart, she knew that the man sprawled out beside Trace was her husband, but her mind wasn't ready to concede the fact.

"Get inside," he bellowed.

A bullet slammed into the white clapboard of the home and sent splinters of wood raining down on Irene's head. The gunshot spurred her into action and she darted into the house to avoid getting shot.

Trace continued exchanging gunfire with the assailants. Beads of sweat popped up on his forehead and he used his sleeve to mop his brow. The morning air felt so still that it seemed to him as if it was holding its breath in anticipation of the outcome of the gunfight. He held the attackers at bay until his rifle ran out of ammunition. The two men must have been counting his shots because they brazenly came out of hiding and started walking toward the house. In a desperate attempt to save himself and his boss's family, Trace sprinted back toward the bunkhouse. Each step of the way was met with gunfire as if the sole purpose of his life was to provide the murderers with a target for practice. He nearly made it to the doorway before the onslaught of bullets cut him down.

Irene sat on the bed with her arms cocooning her small son and daughter. She couldn't get the image of Ike sprawled out on the ground out of her head. He didn't look alive to her, and she wondered if she was now a widow. She became aware of the sudden stillness outside, and felt as frightened by the abrupt silence as she had been by all the shooting. As she waited for whatever happened next, her ragged breathing sounded obtrusive to her ears. She pulled her children in tighter to her and said a silent prayer.

The latch to the bedroom door gave way with a kick, causing the door to swing wildly into the wall. Irene let out a scream and the children began crying as the men barreled into the room. Worse yet, Irene knew the men and why they had come.

"What do you want?" Irene yelled.

"Irene, that's not very hospitable of you," Rusty McClure said with a sneer.

"My God, did you do all of this just because Ike sent you to prison for robbing the trading post? He was the city marshal and it was his job."

"He wasn't the one that spent six years in prison. That gives a man a lot of time to think and build up a good amount of resentment," Mackey McClure responded.

The McClures were fraternal twins born in the year between the births of Ike and his brother, Luka. No one would have ever guessed the McClures were brothers, let alone twins. Rusty was small with strawberry blond hair and Irish features. Mackey stood tall and had brown hair. His long nose was the only thing in his appearance that hinted at his Irish ancestry. The twins never had a father that claimed them, and his identity had for years been the conjecture of many a conversation in Nevada City, Colorado. Miss McClure had never revealed their father's name even to her sons. Without a father to rein the boys in, they had been school bullies and wilder than a March hare. Ike had finally arrested them after they robbed a trading post on the outskirts of Nevada City. They had ended up in the Colorado State Penitentiary for their crime.

"What are you going to do?" Irene asked as she took a closer look at the brothers.

Prison life had aged the McClures more than the six years they'd been there. Their skin had turned leathery looking and they were dark under the eyes. The brothers hadn't shaved in some time, and both had greasy hair and were covered in dust. Irene recoiled at the thought that they were most likely going to be touching her.

"You might want to come quiet like with us unless you want the children to see," Rusty said.

A chill ran down Irene's spine and she shuddered. Her eyes welled with tears as she realized she was about to die. "I'll do whatever you want, but please don't hurt my children," she pleaded.

"That sounds like a fair compromise. Come with us," Mackey said.

Irene hugged her children and kissed them each on top of the head. "You two stay in here and be quiet. Don't leave this room until I come to get you. Do you understand?"

The children were squalling, but obediently nodded their heads.

With a sigh that sounded like death itself, Irene stood and marched out of the room without looking back at her children. She couldn't bear to see their frightened faces another moment. The brothers followed closely behind her, and when she reached the front room, Rusty grabbed her from behind and slung her to the floor. As he began ripping off her clothes, Irene clenched her teeth together, determined not to scream. She scrunched her eyes shut and prayed in an attempt to block out all the pain and humiliation. As Rusty raped her, she fought the urge to vomit from the piglike smell and grunting of her attacker. After Rusty finished his assault, he leered down at Irene before he climbed off her. His brother took his place. Irene prayed so intently that she was barely cognizant of the switch. She knew the end was near and began reciting the Lord's Prayer aloud. When Mackey started making his final moans, Rusty pulled out his Bowie knife and made a quick slash across Irene's throat. In her last thought before her life ended, she wondered who would raise her children. Blood shot into the air and Mackey had to roll away to keep from getting splattered.

"Damn, you could have waited until I finished," Mackey cursed.

"You did your business. Quit your complaining," Rusty replied.

"What now?"

"I'm going to kill the kids."

"Don't you think we ought to let them live?"

"They'd just be orphans anyway. We're doing them a favor."

"Killing children is pure evil. You're liable to have everybody in the Montana Territory after us for doing that. I don't know about this."

"Of course you don't. That's why I'm doing it. We need to get to town and find Luka. The sooner we get him killed, the sooner we can get out of here and the better off we'll be. The Gunther brothers won't ever mess with us again."

Chapter 2

Bozeman, Montana Territory

Luka Gunther was almost home from his nearly two-hundred-mile journey to Fort Benton. He was more than ready to get his butt off the hard board seat and get back to work. He'd traveled to the fort in a specially made wagon to get a load of goods to resupply the trading post he and his brother, Ike, owned. The supplies came by steamboat up the Missouri River. A trip to Helena would have been quicker, but the prices tended to vary wildly for goods shipped up the Montana Trail, and Luka preferred to know what he was going to pay for his merchandise.

The brothers grew up in Nevada City, Colorado, and after they had returned from the War of the Rebellion, Ike had served as the city marshal with Luka as his deputy. By the time Ike's first term ended, their parents had died and the men were tired of dealing with the drunken miners of mostly Irish decent. Luka, along with Ike, and Ike's wife and children, had moved to Bozeman in the Montana Territory to start a new life. Luka managed the trading post while Ike ran their ranch. The arrangement worked well, with Luka selling supplies to the area ranchers and miners headed to Virginia City while Ike provided them with beef. The men had prospered in their new life, and were happy to have left Colorado behind them.

Ike and Luka's resemblance was about the only thing the two men had in common. Anyone could tell that the two were obviously brothers with their prominent foreheads, square jaws, and thin lips. Descendants of working-class Germans, they had broad shoulders and stout frames. Luka stood an inch taller at an even six feet, and his brown hair was wavy, but otherwise, even their walks and mannerisms were the same. Ike had turned thirty-four years of age earlier in the year, and Luka was now thirty-two. Temperament was where the brothers veered in different directions. Ike was quick to anger and would say whatever came to mind. He tended to rub people the wrong way if he didn't agree with their opinions. Luka was just the opposite in personality. He was slow to anger and made good first impressions. After he had completed his time serving in the war and being a deputy, he'd had his fill of guns, and only owned a shotgun for protection at the store and on his trips. Somehow, despite their differences, the brothers got along well and usually only argued for the sake of a good argument.

As Luka neared Bozeman, he caught a whiff of smoke. He turned onto the main street and saw the smoldering remains of his trading post. His heart began thumping in his chest, and he rubbed his hand across his mouth in disbelief. So much hard work had been reduced to nothing more than charred remains that now assaulted his nostrils. A few men were standing around, keeping an eye on the fire to make sure that it didn't spread to any of the other buildings in town. Luka spotted his clerk, Jeb Dole, and jumped off the wagon and ran to him.

"Jeb, what happened? How did the fire start?" Luka asked, disbelief and shock in his voice.

"It's the darndest thing. A couple of men were in the store asking for you and then not an hour later a fire

TRAIL TO YESTERDAY • 8

started in the back. Makes me wonder now if they didn't have something to do with it," Jeb replied.

"What men? What did they want?"

"They asked to see you. I told them you were gone and I didn't know when you would be back since the steamboat gets delayed sometimes. They said they wished they could stay . . ."

"What men?" Luka asked impatiently.

"Said they were the McClure brothers and that they were real sorry they couldn't stay around and give you a proper greeting."

Luka closed his eyes and lifted his head toward the heavens. His legs felt weak and he fought the urge to go sit down. He and Ike had been butting heads with the McClure brothers since their first days of elementary school. When Luka took a moment to collect himself, it dawned on him that the brothers surely had paid Ike a visit, too. A foreboding came over him and he feared for the safety of his brother and family.

"I need to borrow your horse to go check on Ike. The McClures most definitely burned the trading post and I worry they might have done the same to the ranch. They hate Ike and me," Luka said.

"Sure, help yourself. He's right over there," Jeb said and pointed toward his gelding.

"One more thing, Jeb – would you be so kind as to take care of my team of horses and the wagon? I really need to go check on Ike."

"You know you can count on me."

With a nod of his head, Luka sprinted toward the doctor's office. He burst into the building, startling Dr. Faulk and causing him to drop a vial of medicine.

"Damn it, what in darnation is your big hurry?" the doctor growled. He ran his hand through the side of his gray hair and then pulled off his spectacles to peer at Luka.

"I need you to come with me to Ike's ranch," Luka responded.

"What's the problem?"

"As I'm sure you're aware, my trading post just burned down and I fear harm may have come to Ike, too."

"You go on and check first. You can come and get me if I'm needed. I'm not in the habit of making needless house calls."

"I'll pay you double whether you are needed or not, but you're coming with me whether I have to drag you all the way there by rope or of your own accord."

The doctor hastily returned his glasses to his head and let out a huff. "Very well, then. You go on and I'll come as soon as I get my horse saddled."

Luka gave the doctor a skeptical look as he pondered whether to believe him.

"You have my word. Get going if you're in such an all-fire hurry," the doctor said.

"Thank you. I do appreciate it," Luka said before departing.

Luka raced out and mounted the horse. With five miles to cover, he put the gelding into a lope. As he rode, his chest felt so tight from worrying that he wondered if he might suffocate, and his mind ran wild with a hundred different scenarios of what lay ahead of him. When the ranch came into view, Luka started to relax. The place hadn't been burned to the ground. He wondered if maybe all his fears had been for naught. His brief moment of optimism quickly ended with the sight of a body in the yard. He kicked the horse into a gallop for the remainder of the journey.

The sight of the five bodies sprawled out in the yard in grotesque and unnatural looking positions caused Luka to look away from the horrific scene. He jumped off the horse and ran into the house. The first thing that his eyes fell upon was Irene's naked body. Luka could feel his stomach coming up into his throat, and he covered his mouth in an attempt to will it back down. With the hope of finding the children still safe, he ran toward the bedrooms. Little Ike and Marcy were sprawled out on the bed with a bullet in each of their foreheads.

Luka couldn't force down the vomit any longer. He made a dash for outdoors and slid to his knees in the grass. His body felt as if it had turned against him, and he puked until he swore he would die. When the retching finally stopped, he dropped onto his back and stared up at the sky. If he could have willed his heart to stop, he gladly would have died there on the spot with the rest of his family. As he closed his eyes, he tried to clear his head of the macabre scene he'd just witnessed. The attempt to find some peace of mind failed. He felt flushed and sweat beaded up on his forehead. Just as he was thinking that he might get sick again, he heard a moan.

The sound caused Luka to jump to his feet and run toward the bodies in the yard. As he neared Ike, his brother moaned again. Luka dropped to the ground and lifted Ike's head.

"Ike, can you hear me?" Luka asked.

Ike didn't respond and showed no signs that he had heard the words. As Luka cradled Ike's head, he noticed the pumpknot on his brother's forehead and found the injury curious. He ripped Ike's shirt open to see the gunshot wounds. Two bullet holes to the chest, nearly three inches apart, oozed a small amount of blood. Luka untied the kerchief around his neck and applied pressure to the wounds as he awaited the doctor's arrival.

Dr. Faulk arrived fifteen minutes later.

"It's about time you got here," Luka hollered.

The doctor looked around the yard at the carnage, ignoring Luka's comment. "Is anybody else alive?" he asked.

"I don't think so, but I haven't checked for pulses. Irene and the children are dead."

Dr. Faulk winced as if he'd shut his finger in a drawer. He nodded his head solemnly and climbed down from his horse. "Let's get Ike into the house."

The men carried Ike into the home to his and Irene's bedroom. A single groan was the only sound Ike made when they stretched him out onto the bed. Dr. Faulk returned to his horse for his bag and paused in the front room to glance at Irene. The ghastly sight caused the doctor to turn an ashen color. He found a quilt to cover her and then darted away to attend to Ike.

"Go check for a pulse on your ranch hands. We wouldn't want to leave any of them out there to suffer in the sun if they're alive," Dr. Faulk instructed.

While Luka went to check on the men, the doctor cut away Ike's shirt and checked for exit wounds. One of the bullets had made a clean exit, but the one nearest to the lung had remained inside the body. Frothy blood around Ike's nose and mouth informed the doctor that Ike's lung had probably been injured. He retrieved his stethoscope and listened to the chest. Ike's breathing actually sounded pretty good, all things considered. His heartbeat was weak.

Luka returned to the bedroom. "The rest of the men are all dead," he said.

"Ike has a bullet still in him that I'm going to leave alone. I believe it pierced the lung and I'm liable to do more damage than good by trying to get it out. His breathing isn't bad. I think the lung has sealed itself."

The doctor retrieved a pair of forceps and drenched them in carbolic acid before probing the wounds. He pulled a piece of shirt out of one of the bullet holes and dropped it onto the nightstand. After he was satisfied he'd removed all the foreign material from the wounds, he doused them with the carbolic acid before applying bandages. Afterward, he lit a candle and held it in front of Ike's face as he pried open his eyes.

"I've done all I can do," Dr. Faulk said before blowing out the candle. "Ike has lost a lot of blood and his heart sounds weak. I think the lung will be fine, but he has a long ways to go. He could recover or he could waste away. His eyes reacted to light, but to have a lump like that, he had to really whack his head. He might never wake up. I just don't know."

Luka rubbed his index finger across his lower lip. "I see. Well, it's better than already being dead," he said.

"I guess you'll need five adult coffins and two for children. I'll see to it that they get made. When I get back to Bozeman, I'll send some men out here to help you dig graves, too. You have enough on your hands without having to dig seven graves."

"Thank you, doctor. I appreciate your help."

"I'll bring my wife and a preacher with me in the morning. She can dress Irene proper and then we can get them buried. I'm truly sorry for your losses."

"It takes some vile men to do what happened here." Luka's voice had a distant quality to it, and he stared out the window as if his mind wasn't really engaged in the conversation.

"Yes, it does. I'll send the sheriff out here, too. Maybe he can find the men that performed this atrocity."

"If he doesn't, I will once I can get free of here – I promise you that. We should have shot the McClures a long time ago."

"Some men's only purpose in life is to provide for a good killing."

"Will you take Jeb's horse back to town with you?"

"Sure I will. Are you going to be all right?"

Luka turned his head to make eye contact with the doctor. "I don't have much choice in the matter. I have to save my brother. He's been there since the day I came into this world, and I'm not even close to ready to go on without him."

"I'll help you carry Irene into the bedroom with the children. There's no need to leave her in the middle of the floor. That poor woman suffered an ignoble death. Her last moments on earth had to be pure hell."

Luka nodded his head and the first tears came. He tried to hold them in, but a sob escaped his lips and then uncontrollable crying followed that he couldn't stop until it had run its course. He turned his head away from the doctor in embarrassment. It had been years since he'd cried and the feeling felt as foreign to him as a woman's touch. When he finally caught his breath, he jumped up and headed for the front of the house.

The doctor helped Luka carry Irene into the bedroom and then he covered the children's bodies with a blanket before taking his leave.

Luka walked into the kitchen and found the whiskey bottle that Ike stored in the cabinet there. He pulled the cork out with his teeth and then took two longs swigs, enjoying the slow burn into his stomach. After plugging the bottle, he collapsed into a kitchen chair. In the past, he'd had some bad and lonely days over a woman he loved with all his heart, but those days now seemed like nothing compared to the hollow feeling he felt inside of him now.

As Dr. Faulk had promised, four men arrived from town with shovels to help dig the graves. They assisted Luka in laying out the seven burial spots and then got to digging.

Sheriff Garr showed up at the ranch in the afternoon to survey the carnage. Luka climbed out of the waist deep hole he was digging and mopped the sweat from his brow before shaking the sheriff's hand. Sheriff Garr had a reputation as a no-nonsense man and he wasted no time before asking to see what had happened. As Luka led the sheriff around to show him the bodies and where they had been found, he tried to remain stoic, but the sight of Irene and the children caused him to bolt from the room and leave the sheriff on his own. A couple of minutes later, the sheriff joined Luka in the front room, looking as pale as a ghost. Luka didn't know Sheriff Garr all that well, but the man had seemed genuinely horrified that such a heinous crime had been committed in his county. He promised Luka that he'd form a posse to track the McClures to hell and back if necessary to bring them to justice.

After the sheriff had gone and the graves were dug, Luka forced himself to scrub Irene's blood from the floor. His already empty stomach was the only thing that prevented him from getting sick again. The quantity of blood looked enormous and took two buckets of water to complete the cleaning. Even then, the boards would always carry the stain of what had happened upon them.

That night proved to be a longest one of Luka's life. Though he was exhausted from digging the graves, he felt too distraught and grief-stricken to sleep much, and the few times he did dose off, Ike's moaning would immediately wake him. As he lay in the bed, he couldn't help but to relive all the dustups he and Ike had had with Rusty and Mackey over the years. He still couldn't fathom how the McClures could be so bitter as to commit such atrocities nor could he believe that they'd come all the way to the Montana Territory to act upon them. While it wasn't a secret that Ike and Luka had moved to Bozeman, it wasn't as if that many people knew of their whereabouts either. Luka guessed gossip in a small town had eventually made it common knowledge. Before his days were done, he planned to give the folks of Nevada City a whole lot more to talk about if the sheriff couldn't find the McClure brothers.

Chapter 3

Nevada City, Colorado

As a gold miner sauntered down an aisle in O'Sullivan's General Store, he paused to slip a couple of cans of beans into his oversized coat. Alannah O'Sullivan had been working in the store for her parents since she was a teenager and had become a sleuth when it came to shoplifting. While she restocked the shelves, she spied the miner stealing the food but decided to hold her tongue for the moment. In the past, every time she confronted a customer, her daddy would intervene on her behalf. His efforts to protect his daughter had gotten him pistol-whipped once, and beaten up twice. Alannah had no intentions of ever letting that happen again. She glanced toward the counter and saw her mother still standing there. Her father had yet to return from the back of the store where he worked on the ledgers.

The miner walked up to the front of the store and paid Mrs. O'Sullivan for a plug of tobacco before leaving. As soon as the door closed, Alannah raced behind the counter and fetched the shotgun the family kept there for protection. She rushed outside before her mother even realized what was happening, and found the miner walking away down the boardwalk. The unmistakable clicks of Alannah pulling back both hammers on the gun caused the miner to stop in his tracks.

"Don't turn around or I'll blow you straight to hell," Alannah warned in her Irish lilted voice. "I want you to reach into your coat and slowly place those cans of beans onto the boardwalk. If you don't, I'm going to let my shotgun open them while they're still in your pocket. Wouldn't that be a mess mixed in with all your blood – and what a smell? People will think you messed yourself from fear of a woman."

The miner slowly moved his arm toward his pocket and retrieved the two cans. He gently set them down on the boardwalk.

"Don't come back into our store unless you plan to pay for what you take. Now get out of here," Alannah barked.

"Damn old spinster," the miner groused as he hastily made his retreat.

By the time Alannah uncocked the shotgun, her parents had joined her.

"What did you do this time?" Connor O'Sullivan demanded in his heavy Irish brogue.

"I got our goods back without your help. You don't need any more beatings," Alannah remarked.

"You could have gotten yourself killed over a couple of cans of beans. I can always get more beans, but not another daughter."

Alannah sighed with disgust. "You have enough daughters that you wouldn't have missed one, and I would have sent him straight to hell if he'd gone for his gun."

"Alannah O'Sullivan, such talk from a lady," Nora O'Sullivan chided her daughter.

"Would you really want to go to the Kingdom of Heaven with such a mark on your slate? Killing a man for beans would be a great sin. Honestly, Alannah, I don't know what you were thinking," Connor said.

"Somebody has to be the law around here. That useless city marshal sure isn't going to protect us."

"Young lady, that is neither here nor there. Get back into the store and act like a proper lady," her father ordered.

Being called "young lady" hit Alannah wrong. After all, she had turned thirty years old this year. And while she did still live with her parents, she was certainly tired of them treating her as if she were still a child. She took a deep breath, pulling her shoulders back as she did so, and shoved the shotgun into her father's hands before marching off down the street.

Alannah's mind raced all over the place. She had three sisters and two brothers, and it seemed to her that her parents should have had all of their bossing out of the way by now. And with all her siblings married to other Irish, there was a plethora of grandchildren to boss around if her parents still felt the need. She hated family gatherings where her sisters always asked if she had a new beau, and would ramble on about their children for hours. Whenever the opportunity arose, Alannah would sneak off and play with her nieces and nephews to avoid all of the adults.

She'd heard that men around town took pleasure in calling her the oldest virgin in Nevada City even though she knew that wasn't true. There were plenty of old maids around there. She might be a maiden, but she wasn't that old. From time to time, she still had male callers, but none of them ever caught her fancy. She gave her heart away as a teenager, and no matter how much time had passed to let the memory fade, no one ever measured up to Luka Gunther. They had courted for years, but her parents never liked Luka because he was Lutheran and they were devout Catholics. The couple had fought about religion a thousand times. She had tried to get him to convert to Catholicism, but Luka had always refused. He'd gone as far as agreeing that their children would be raised Catholic, but that had never been good enough for Alannah. She knew she would never have heard the end of it from her parents, and what they thought had always carried the weight of the world with her. Letting Luka go would be the one thing in life that she never truly got over.

As Alannah passed the jail, she got all fired up again about the law in Nevada City. The place had gone to hell in a handbasket ever since Ike Gunther's term as city marshal had ended. Truth be told, the only reason Ike got elected was that nobody ran against him. The Irish were loyal to their own, and Ike most likely would have lost if he'd run again anyway. Grady Kelly, the current city marshal, would have probably beaten him. Marshal Kelly was about useless. He protected his cronies and let the town run wild. The law-abiding citizens were mostly on their own. On most nights, Grady could be found in one of the saloons getting drunk with all the miners.

All of Alannah's reminiscing over Ike and Luka led her to think back to their school days together. The Gunthers had always been outcast because of their German ancestry. They stood out like sore thumbs amongst all the Irish children. They even sounded different. While the Irish children talked with lilts and brogues, the Gunthers tended to attack a consonant like a butcher taking a meat clever to a side of beef. Their mother could only speak enough English to manage to go alone to the store. Alannah had always felt a kinship with the brothers. Her family was one of the few Black Irish in the area, and she had been painfully aware of the difference in her appearance to that of the other Irish children. Her hair was wavy and nearly black, and she had dark eyes and a dark complexion. Children had teased her over her appearance, and she had made more than one of them cry for their rude behavior.

Alannah let out sigh, tired of all her pondering about the past. She looked up and down the street to see if anybody was watching her. Finding the coast clear, she darted into an alley and entered Clancy's Saloon through the back door into the room where all of the liquor and beer was stored. The place was an assault to the nose with its menagerie of smells. The beer, whiskey, and dankness all combined for an aroma that Alannah had never experienced anywhere else in her life. She slipped into a side room where the saloon girls took respite during their long shifts of serving customers booze and other sinful pleasures.

Betty Anne sat at the table, smoking a cigarette. She was a petite blond with great big blue eyes and a cute face. Her honey-soaked voice could get men to spend money like no other saloon girl in town. She looked up in surprise at seeing Alannah. "What brings you in here at this time of day?" she asked.

"I've had another fight with my parents. I need a beer," Alannah said.

"Say no more." Betty Anne jumped up and disappeared from the room.

Alannah secretly loved the taste of beer. After all, she was Irish to the core. She knew if her parents ever found out that she imbibed alcohol, they would disown her. Luka had introduced her to beer on one of their wilder nights on the town. She had instantly loved the bitter taste. After he moved away, she had gone years without drinking a brew. One day she had been cutting through the alley and had struck up a conversation with a saloon girl named Wanda. One thing led to another, and now Alannah made the occasional trip to the back of Clancy's when she needed a beer or some company. She liked the saloon girls. Most of them were nice and they were never judgmental. They could relate to being outcasts and were good listeners by nature.

Betty Anne returned and set the beer in front of Alannah before taking a seat. "What is it this time?" she asked.

The beer looked so inviting that Alannah took her first sip before responding. She recounted all that had gone on at the store and the treatment she had received from her parents. "That's about the long and short of it," she said to end her story.

"Alannah, you're a grown woman. You need a place of your own. Your parents are always going to treat you like a child as long as you live under their roof. It's time to be independent. I bet they'll change how they treat you once you're gone," Betty Anne said.

"Do you really think it would help?"

"I do. Your parents have never changed how they treat you because nothing else ever changed. You're still the daughter in the bedroom down the hall."

"My parents are in their fifties now, but they were always old for their ages and so rigid. You do make good points. Maybe I'm too set in my ways too to ever live on my own now, though. I've never known anything else but that bedroom of mine," Alannah said and took a big gulp of beer, getting foam on her upper lip.

"Nonsense. I can't believe you didn't move out years ago."

Shaking her head, Alannah pondered the statement. "I guess I never thought I had a reason to leave home.

When you think about it, it does make me seem like the child my parents still see me as being."

"There's nothing like the present to make a change. You might have a few more gentlemen callers if they didn't have to meet mom and dad at the door."

Alannah let out a giggle. "I'm afraid I am hopeless on that count. That train has come and is long gone."

"You could become a saloon girl and get caught up real quick," Betty Anne teased.

Giggling hysterically, Alannah couldn't catch her breath and snorted. When she finally stopped laughing, she said, "You're a good friend, Betty Anne. You are just what I needed today. But as for me being a saloon girl, those prospectors would think finding gold in one of those mines is easy compared to finding a tunnel of gold on me." She slapped the table and cackled.

Chapter 4

Bozeman, Montana Territory

As the sky began to turn pink on the eastern horizon on the morning after the murders, Luka checked on Ike again. He held the oil lamp in front of his brother's face and studied him. Ike looked as gray as the morning, and his breathing sounded shallow and ragged. Luka wondered if at any moment, he would see Ike draw his last breath.

While Luka wasn't a nervous man by nature, the thought of losing Ike caused his hands to tremble, and he continuously rubbed his forehead. With Ike being two years older, he had always been the leader. Sometimes his brother's bossiness had vexed Luka, but truth be told, he wasn't sure he knew how to exist anymore without him. Over the years, he'd gotten used to being the follower. The only time their positions had been reversed was during the war, when Luka's cooler head had gotten him promoted over his brother. That had been an interesting time, and the memory actually brought a smile to Luka's face as he thought back to giving his brother orders. From that military promotion, he had learned that he could actually be an effective leader when he needed to be.

Whether Ike lived or not, the ranch would always be lacking without Irene there to spice up the day. She was the glue that kept everything together. When they had all moved to the territory, they had struggled to get the ranch up and going. She had been the one to come up with the idea of the trading post. The store had been so successful that the profits from it had allowed them to spend the money to make the ranch profitable. On the personal side, Irene had always treated Luka as if he were her little brother instead of a third wheel she'd inherited when she married Ike. He loved her dearly.

Luka didn't dare let his mind drift to thoughts of Little Ike and Marcy. For a long time now, he'd come to the conclusion that being their uncle was the closet he would ever come to having his own family. He'd always spoiled them rotten, and they had adored him. Nothing would ever be the same again.

After wiping off Ike's face with a wet rag, Luka went to the kitchen and managed to get down a cup of coffee. He'd yet to eat since returning to Bozeman, but the idea of food repulsed him. As he poured a second cup, Dr. Faulk, his wife, the Lutheran preacher, and a couple of men to help with the burials arrived at the ranch.

"Good morning," Luka greeted in a voice that sounded friendlier than he felt.

"How's our patient?" Dr. Faulk asked, skipping formalities.

"He's still alive is about all I know."

"Let's go have a look."

Dr. Faulk and his wife followed Luka to the bedroom where the doctor promptly began his examination. He pried open Ike's eyes and did a quick check with the candle before retrieving his stethoscope. After carefully listening to Ike's heart and lungs, the doctor slowing removed the instrument from his ears, and looked at Luka. "His heart sounds about the same, but his breathing is shallow. If he doesn't regain consciousness so that we can make him take deep breaths, he'll get pneumonia. His eyes are still reacting to light, but we need more than that."

Luka sighed loudly and nodded his head.

"Why don't you take Trisha and show her where Irene and the children's clothes are so that she can dress them?"

"Mrs. Faulk, are you sure you want to do this? It's a gruesome sight," Luka said.

"I've been helping my husband for thirty years. There isn't anything that I haven't seen by now. While I don't confess to being so callous that the sights do not trouble me, I've learned how to live with the horrors the human race can perpetrate upon itself," Mrs. Faulk replied.

"All right, then." Luka tried not to look dismayed by her long-winded reply.

After Luka had showed Mrs. Faulk where the clothes and the bodies were located, Dr. Faulk joined them.

"I'll help Trisha if you want to show the men to the other bodies to get them into the coffins," the doctor said.

Luka walked outside and saw the buckboard wagon on which the men had arrived. The coffins were stacked high upon it and secured with ropes. The morbid sight gave him a chill and he shuddered. He led the men to the barn where he had dragged the bodies. The wagon was moved over to the barn and the men made quick work of placing the corpses into the wooden caskets and nailing down the lids. As they were finishing their work, it dawned on Luka that the ranch hands were from all parts of the country and that Irene was the only one that probably had a clue on who to notify of their deaths. He guessed their families would find out when they got around to writing the dead men.

By the time Luka returned to the home, the doctor and his wife had dressed the bodies of Irene and the children.

"Would you like some time alone with them?" Mrs. Faulk asked.

Luka thought about the question a moment before deciding he didn't think he could bear to see them again in their condition. Nice clothes wouldn't make the holes in the children's heads go away or hide that Irene's head was nearly severed. "No, I just want to get them buried," he replied.

The family members were put into the coffins and then all of the caskets were carted to the makeshift graveyard. Reverend Dobbs knew the family from church, and talked glowingly of them before leading the attendees in reciting Psalms 23. With the short service concluded the reverend shook Luka's hand and offered his condolences.

Dr. Faulk, his wife, and Reverend Dobbs took their leave. As soon as they were gone, Luka began helping the men with the arduous task of scooping the dirt back into the seven holes in the ground. By the time they finished, all of the men were covered in sweat and tired. Luka gave the men his word that he would pay them as soon as he made it back to town to get some money out of the bank, and the men seemed satisfied with his promise.

Once the laborers had departed, Luka stood in the yard and stared at the seven mounds before his eyes. For the first time since arriving home, the shock of what had happened had worn off enough that anger came over Luka. In his fury, he stood there with his fists balled up and his whole body trembling. He swore that if the law didn't bring justice to the family, the vengeance would be his.

Luka walked back to the house and gathered up all the bloody clothes and blankets. After carrying them out into the yard and dousing them with kerosene, he tossed a match onto the pile. As he watched the cloth burn, his anger still coursed through his blood. He marched back into the home and retrieved Ike's revolver and rifle. If he had to be the one to find justice, he'd better be damned sure he could still shoot a gun.

The target practice didn't go well. He was so worked up that his concentration was lacking and his shots were all over the place. Finally, he gave up in disgust and went back inside the home.

After dropping onto a bed, Luka prayed, "God, please give me the strength to carry on. I don't think I can do it without you. And please let Ike recover. I need my brother." He dropped into his first sound sleep since his return home.

Just as it neared suppertime, Luka awakened from his slumber. His belly growled, and he realized he needed a meal. He decided to check on Ike before he fixed himself something to eat. With the curtains pulled shut, there remained just enough light in the bedroom to see Ike's features. The sight of Ike staring up at the ceiling caused Luka to jump in surprise.

"Ike, can you hear me?" Luka asked. He hustled over to the window and threw the curtains open.

Ike looked at his brother with an expression so void of comprehension that Luka thought Ike must now be addle-brained.

"Ike, say something."

"What happened?" Ike whispered.

"You got shot and must have hit your head when you collapsed."

Ike glanced back at the ceiling. His blank expression slowly evolved into a look of recollection, and he nodded his head. "Where's Irene?" he asked, his voice rising in panic.

For a brief moment, Luka planned to lie, but his expression must have given him away because Ike looked horrified. Luka quickly realized that he had to tell the truth since he sure as hell wasn't going to be able to produce Irene. "Ike, you're the only one on the ranch that survived."

"The kids, too?"

Luka nodded his head.

A wail came out of Ike like nothing Luka had ever heard in his life. It sounded as if every sorrow ever perpetrated on humankind was rolled up into the howl.

"Ike, I'm so sorry. I wish there was something I could have done. I got here too late."

"Did they rape her?"

Luka looked down and rubbed his forehead. "Yes."

"My family is gone – my whole family. And Irene had to suffer that humiliation before she died. Those men are no better than pigs. Why would they do this to us? Do you know who did it?"

"The McClures did it. They were in town asking for me. I guess they were afraid to stay around after doing what they did out here. Jeb told them he didn't know when I'd be back."

Ike turned his head away from his brother and closed his eyes. "Just leave me be. I'm going to die now."

Luka squatted down next to the bed and put his hand on Ike. "You have to get well so that we can find those bastards and make them pay. And you have to get well for me. I don't have a soul in this world if I lose you. Do it for me if for nothing else. I'm afraid to be alone."

"I don't know if I have the will to live."

"I'm going to go get you some water. You need to drink. Dr. Faulk said to take deep breaths, too. It'll keep you from getting pneumonia. I'll be right back."

Luka left and soon returned with a pitcher of water and a glass. Ike greedily drank down two glasses and then gulped air to catch his breath.

"That's the best water I ever tasted. I was dry," Ike said.

"Good, you needed that."

"I don't know which hurts worse – my head or trying to breathe."

"I'm just glad you're alive to feel anything. I'm going to go make you some bone broth. You need nourishment. I'll be right back."

Luka went to the kitchen and lit a fire in the stove. Years of being a bachelor had made him proficient in cooking. He put a pan of water onto the stovetop before heading to the smokehouse and retrieving a knucklebone saved for just such occasions. While he waited for the water to come to a boil, he scarfed down some bread with jam to thwart his hunger.

The water seemed to be taking forever to come to boil, and as Luka sat at the table, he thought about Ike. For the first time since the shootings, he had some hope that his brother would live. While he doubted Ike would ever be the same, Luka was willing to take whatever he got as long as his brother lived. He was determined to do his damndest to make it happen.

Once the bone had finally cooked, Luka poured the broth into a bowl, grabbed a spoon, and hurried back to the bedroom. Ike was staring up at the ceiling again when he entered the room. A trail of tears ran down his cheeks that he quickly wiped away with his hand. He struggled to sit up to eat so Luka helped prop his brother up with the aid of some pillows. The exertion caused Ike to groan in pain, but he never complained.

"I'll feed myself, if you don't mind," Ike said when Luka went to spoon some broth out of the bowl.

"That suits me just fine. I don't see myself as your nursemaid anyway," Luka said in his first attempt at some humor.

Ike took each spoonful slowly and deliberately. While his meal would never measure up against one of Irene's feasts, the broth tasted pretty darn good. When he had nearly consumed all of the broth, he tipped up the bowl and drank the last of its contents. "I guess Irene isn't here to chide me about my manners anymore," he said, his voice a mixture of sadness and irony.

"No, but I'm sure she's looking down at you and shaking her head that way she always did," Luka responded.

"I sure hope so."

"Ike, I promise you that if the sheriff doesn't bring the McClures in, we will. I'll track them until my last days on earth if I have to."

Ike leaned his head back against the pillows and grimaced as he took a deep breath. "Yes, we will. I'll live for no other reason than vengeance."

Chapter 5

Montana Trail, Montana Territory

After the McClure brothers had set fire to the trading post, they hightailed it in a southwesterly direction across the Montana Territory. The brothers had two sound horses apiece that they'd stolen so that they could keep the animals fresh if a posse came in hot pursuit. When they reached Virginia City, they never even bothered to stop for a beer. Money was running low anyway. As the sun disappeared over the western horizon on the third day of hard riding, the brothers reached the Montana Trail. They made camp, figuring their worries were over as far as being captured by the law.

The Montana Trail was a well-worn wagon road that stretched from Salt Lake City to Fort Benton. Most of the supplies used by the miners and settlers of the Montana Territory arrived on wagons pulled by mules or oxen via the trail. No posse would be able to track the brothers on the heavily used path. Best of all, the trail was ripe for robberies. Settlers headed north to start a new life would make for easy pickings. And if the brothers were bold enough, an attack on a team of muleskinners and bullwhackers returning from delivering their goods could make the McClures rich.

As the brothers sat around the campfire, Rusty used his teeth to yank off a bite of jerky. With his mouth still full of meat, he began to speak. "We're safe now, and we never even caught sight of a posse. That proved easier than I even expected. The Gunther brothers don't seem so tough now."

"I don't know. We made a mistake and should have made sure they were both around before we killed Ike. I fear we'll be looking over our shoulder for Luka for the rest of our days," Mackey said.

"You're right that we made a mistake, but who would have guessed that one of them would be gone. I wanted them both dead, but I ain't worried about Luka. Ike was the mean one. Luka don't have it in him to find us."

"I don't know about that. Ike might have been the hotheaded one, but when Luka made his mind up about something, he stuck to it. Remember that time you stole his marbles. He waited a month for the right opportunity to give you a beating."

"Of course you wouldn't agree with me. You never do. And you had to bring up that old memory. The only reason Luka whipped me was that those damn Germans have heads made of steel. I punched him right in the temple and he never even flinched. A normal boy would have been knocked silly."

"So you say. I think they just come from tough stock. I always heard that their daddy could prospect with the best of the Irishmen. Also heard that none of them ever gave him any lip. Word was that he could be mean in a fight." Mackey took a sip of coffee and eyed his brother over the brim of the cup to see if he'd succeeded in riling him.

"I hated their old man. I swear he always stared at us as if he hated us or something. I never did nothing to him."

"I'm sure Ike and Luka filled him in on all our shenanigans. We weren't ever going to win any school awards."

Mackey had accomplished his goal in getting his brother all worked up. Rusty bit off a chunk of hardtack as if it had affronted him.

"We didn't have no choice but to be mean. Nobody was ever going to call me a bastard twice. Ma made life damn hard for us with what she did," Rusty complained.

"We wouldn't be here if Ma hadn't done what she did. Did you ever think of that? She did the best she could, and she always had a roof over our heads and food on the table."

"This conversation is pointless, and I'm through talking." Rusty, in his state of agitation, gulped his coffee and burnt his mouth. He cussed a blue streak and slung the cup into the brush.

"If you ever want to drink coffee again, you'll have to crawl around in there and find your cup. You ain't sharing with me."

"Oh, shut up for a while," Rusty yelled. He stormed out of the camp and disappeared into the tree line.

When Rusty returned a good fifteen minutes later, he sheepishly retrieved his cup and poured himself some coffee. He gave Mackey a stare that all but dared his brother to open his mouth.

"So what's our plan from here?" Mackey asked.

"I figure we'd head south down this wagon trail tomorrow. Just go at a walk to let the horses recover. We can have our eyes peeled for any settlers off on their own that we can rob. We need some money for supplies and ammunition. Once we have that, we'll find us a good place to ambush one of the freighters returning to Salt Lake."

Mackey squirmed his butt uneasily on the ground. "They say those muleskinners and bullwhackers are a mean lot. We'll be outnumbered to boot. I don't know about this."

"Who is "they"? A bullet kills those old codgers the same as it does anybody else. If we find the right freighter, we'll be rich. Stop your worrying."

"If you say so," Mackey said with no conviction in his voice.

"Think what we'd be able to buy for Ma with that money. She could have some nice things for once in her life."

"I hope you're right. It'd be a pity to get ourselves killed now after serving six years in that hellhole. I'm going to stretch out now. It's been a long three days."

Mackey grabbed his bedroll and stood to unroll it. Once he had it spread on the ground, he carefully smoothed the material until satisfied he'd made a good bed, and then he crawled inside.

"I guess I could use the sleep, too," Rusty said, since he didn't have anyone with whom to carry on a conversation. He dumped his coffee and went to bed.

With morning's first light, Mackey was up and frying the last of the bacon and boiling coffee. He set the cooked bacon in a tin plate and then mixed flour and water into the grease to make some clumpy gravy to dip the hardtack in. The concoction would certainly never rival his ma's milk gravy and biscuits, but it at least made the hard crackers a little more palatable.

Rusty crawled out of his bedroll, poured a cup of coffee, and started heaping the bacon onto his plate. He tended to be surly in the morning, and Mackey usually gave him a wide berth, but he began to fear his brother would take all of the meat.

"If you take one more piece of bacon, you're going to be wearing this boiling gravy. I got to eat, too," Mackey growled.

Rusty eyed his brother warily. Most days, he ordered Mackey around like a puppy, but he'd learned a long time ago not to push his brother when he set his foot down about something. He knew from experience that Mackey could thump him every time. "Sure. I was going to save you your share," he said.

Mackey nodded his head, and retrieved the plate of bacon. The brothers ate in silence without further strife. Once the meal was eaten, they quickly broke camp and were riding on the trail by the time the sun peeked over the horizon.

The brothers had never ridden this trail, and were surprised by the amount of traffic on the path. By noon, they had already met two freighter companies with three wagons each. One of them had teams of mules while the other used oxen. The muleskinners and bullwhackers never bothered to acknowledge the brothers' existence. They seemed too busy cussing at the animals to take time to offer a greeting. Seeing all the settler wagons, the brothers wondered aloud if every family in the country was headed for the Montana Territory. Some of them were in groups of ten to fifteen wagons while others were going it alone.

In midafternoon, the brothers saw a lone wagon with no other travelers in sight.

"They look like they are begging to be robbed," Rusty said, nodding his head toward the wagon coming their way. "We can rob them and ride hard until evening."

"We're not going to harm them, and I mean it," Mackey warned.

"You're awfully bossy today."

"We had our reasons for killing Ike, but we're not going to make a habit out of killing. That's a good way to get our necks stretched. I aim to enjoy spending some of the money we take on this trail on our way to Salt Lake."

"Well, all right then. Let's get to business."

The brothers rode toward the covered wagon as casually as if they were out for a Sunday ride. The couple sitting up on the wagon seat looked to be in their early thirties. From their appearances, they seemed to have come a long ways and endured a good bit of hardship. Their clothes were worn and in need of replacement, and their skin looked browned to the point of being overbaked.

Rusty drew his revolver and pointed it at the man. "This is a robbery. We just want your money and nobody will get hurt," he threatened.

From the way that the man's eyes darted around, Mackey could see that the settler was contemplating reaching for his rifle. Mackey reached for his pistol and pulled back the hammer. "I'm going to kill your wife if you touch that rifle," he warned.

The settler put his hands in the air while his wife started bawling. The commotion caused two children to pop their heads out of the wagon and stare at the two strangers with guns pointed at them.

"The last thing we want to do is hurt anybody, but if you don't give us your money, we'll be forced to burn your wagon. So hand it over and save us all some grief," Rusty said.

The couple remained sitting without uttering a word. They seemed to be too shocked by their ordeal to react. Mackey decided to take matters into his own hands and jumped down from his horse. He marched to the rear of the wagon and climbed into the back end. The boy and girl, probably around seven and eight years old, stared at him with blank expressions.

"Where's the money?" Mackey hollered as he rummaged through the belongings.

The intrusion forced the woman out of her stupor and she climbed into the back of the wagon to protect her children. With a glare that warned Mackey not to touch her babies, she threw open a trunk and began tossing her possessions to the side until she found a leather pouch. She smacked the bag into Mackey's hand. He holstered his revolver and emptied five ten-dollar gold pieces into his hand. After bouncing the coins in his palm a couple of times, Mackey's conscience got the better of him and he returned one of the coins to the pouch. He handed the bag back to the woman and crawled out of the wagon.

"I got the money. Let's get out of here," Mackey said as he mounted his horse.

The brothers put their horses into a lope and headed south. They continued at that pace until the animals were lathered.

When they finally slowed to a walk, Rusty asked, "How much did we get?"

"Forty dollars."

"Not bad. That's more than I figured those sodbusters had. That's enough to get some supplies and cartridges. Our next robbery will be our big payday."

For the rest of the afternoon, the brothers pushed their horses as hard as they dared considering all the traveling they'd done in the last few days. Toward suppertime, they came upon a trading post out in the middle of nowhere that some enterprising entrepreneur had established to take advantage of those that had set out on the trail lacking sufficient provisions.

The old man behind the counter was a colorful sight. He had long gray hair that reached his shoulders and a beard to match. His buckskin outfit was completed with two shoulder-holstered Colts and a cartridge belt brimming with ammunition.

"What can I do for you?" the old man asked in a booming voice.

Rusty ordered cartridges, bacon, hardtack, jerky, coffee, and some other things the brothers would need before they reached civilization. The prices were exorbitant, but there was nothing that could be done about the cost. The old man had a monopoly.

As Mackey paid the bill, the old man said, "You boys had best watch yourselves. Fellows like you two always meet their match and end up dead. You should consider making an honest living while you still have time."

Rusty's mouth dropped open before he recovered from the shock of the statement. "Mind your own damn business or we're liable to rob you," he said.

The old man rested his hands on his two revolvers. "You wouldn't be the first that tried, but none of them have made it out that door alive to tell about it yet."

Mackey scooped up the packages and headed for the door. "Come on," he said.

Once they had mounted their horses, Rusty asked, "Do you believe that old man?"

"Let's get out of here. That man is too smart for his own good, and I don't trust him. He's liable to round up some other old codgers to come after us. Let's ride."

Chapter 6

Nevada City, Colorado

The tension was so thick inside O'Sullivan's General Store that customers would come into the business and nervously shop without having any idea why they suddenly felt anxious. Alannah and her parents were barely on speaking terms, and when they did attempt a conversation, it would always turn into a loud knock-down, drag-out argument. After Alannah had stewed on Betty Anne's advice for a couple of days, she had decided that her friend was right, and made the decision that she was ready to live on her own. Her parents had been horrified by the announcement and had thought the notion to be improper and immoral. They had gone so far as to ban Alannah from moving out of the house. Their demand had so incensed her that she felt more determined than ever to find her own place to live.

Alannah kept glancing at the store clock, wishing that three o'clock would arrive and that the store would have some customers at that time so that she could take her leave without another fight with her parents. She had an appointment with the widow Mrs. Blake to see the house of the old woman's spinster sister, Miss Ryan. Miss Ryan had recently died, and Mrs. Blake seemed anxious to rent out the place.

After much internal debate, Alannah decided that if she was going to go to the trouble of moving out, she needed a place all to herself. She had briefly considered moving into a boarding house, but quickly concluded that that arrangement would not be much different from living with her parents. Someone would always be watching and judging her actions. She was ready for some privacy.

The store was empty of customers at ten minutes until three, and Alannah couldn't wait any longer to leave. She grabbed her shawl and threw it over her shoulders as she made a beeline for the door.

"Alannah, stop. We're a proper family and I forbid you from moving out of our house. We have our reputation to think about. You are not some harlot," Connor O'Sullivan called out to his daughter.

Alannah spun around, dug her fists into her hips, and cast her dark eyes upon her father in a glare that looked lethal. "I am thirty years old, and I am too old to be ordered around like a child. What I'm about to do has no reflection upon the family. I need to live my own life. All I have ever done is live the life you chose for me, and I'm sick and tired of it. And if you would have given Luka Gunther half of a chance, I would have been happily married years ago. By now, I would think it is obvious that I'm not going to be having men line up at my door. I've never known the pleasure of a man and I guess I never will. You're the reason I'm an old maid. I'm leaving now," she fumed.

"Such bawdry talk from you. It might be hard to pay the rent if you don't have a job," her father threatened.

"You do what you think you have to do. You know as well as I do that that old codger Mr. Fitzgerald will hire me tomorrow for his dry goods store. If you want some scandal, wait until he and all the old men that hang out there laugh and point at my behind every time I bend over to stock a shelf." Alannah spun around and disappeared out the door before her father could respond.

In Alannah's state of irritation, she stalked toward the house where she was to meet Mrs. Blake as if she might be a soldier on a mission to save the nation. She found the widow waiting for her in the yard with her arms folded and her foot tapping.

"Good to see you, Alannah," Mrs. Blake greeted in the formal sounding tone she always used.

"Good to see you, too, Mrs. Blake," Alannah replied.

"Let me show you the home." Mrs. Blake led Alannah into the house and gave her a tour. When she finished, she said, "As you can see, the house is in fine shape and furnished. You won't need to buy furniture or anything. The rent is twenty-five dollars a month and payable on the first."

Alannah glanced around the front room one more time. The place reeked with old person smell, and the colors were drab. With a good scrubbing and some fresh paint, the house could be a cozy little place for her to call home. Years of working in a store had made her a tough negotiator. She planned to put her skills to use. "All I can afford is twenty dollars a month. If you need more rent than that, you'll have to find another renter, and I'll have to look elsewhere."

Mrs. Blake peered over her spectacles with her mouth puckered up as if she'd bitten into a persimmon. She had been a widow longer than she had been married and never had children. Over the years, she had become as rigid and humorless as her old maid sister. Alannah thought the widow was trying to get her to falter so she stared back without blinking or speaking.

"Very well, twenty dollars will suffice, but there will be no consorting with men in this house. I have a reputation to keep, and I won't have carnal sin taking place on my property," Mrs. Blake said.

Alannah set her jaw and squeezed her lips together so tightly that they all but disappeared from sight. She'd had about all the condescending lectures she could stand for one day. "I know that you and all the other old ladies gossip about how all the O'Sullivan girls married fine men except for poor Alannah. You sit around and speculate on how I'll end up an old maid just like your sister. I would think that worrying about me entertaining men would be the least of your worries."

Mrs. Blake puffed up like a balloon being filled with air. "Well, back in the day, you were certainly all about town with that German boy. It's not like you haven't had suitors," she retorted.

"That German boy and I broke up about four years ago and he moved to the Montana Territory three years ago. I haven't heard from him since then. I don't think you have to worry about him or anybody else for that matter coming around this place. I seem to have a thing for those German boys and they are slim pickings around here."

"Very well then. Just so we have an understanding." Mrs. Blake held out her hand with the key.

Alannah took the key and retrieved the money from her bag for rent for the remainder of the month. "Thank you, Mrs. Blake. You won't be sorry that you rented to me."

After walking outside, Alannah surveyed the outside of her new residence with a smile. She felt proud that she had accomplished her goal, but her nerves were fraught and she needed some conversation with a friendly face. She headed for the alley behind Clancy's Saloon and slipped into the back. The room for the saloon girls sat empty so she took a seat and waited. Five minutes later, the sound of laughter reached Alannah just before Betty Anne and Wanda entered the room.

The surprise of seeing Alannah sitting in the room caused the girls to stop their giggling. Wanda took one look at Alannah and spun around to go retrieve a beer without so much as saying a word.

Betty Anne plopped down into a chair. "You look frazzled," she said.

"I am," Alannah responded. "And it's all your fault."

"My fault? What did I do?"

"I just rented Miss Ryan's old house."

Betty Anne let out a squeal and reached across the table to grab Alannah's hands. "Good for you. You've needed your own place forever."

Wanda returned with a beer and set it on the table.

"Thank you, Wanda. I don't know if I should have gotten my own place or not. My family is ready to disown me, and Daddy even threatened to fire me."

"Oh, he's just saying that to try to get his way," Wanda said. "You should have told him you would join us as a saloon girl if he did."

"I told him I'd go work for Fitzgerald if I couldn't work in the store."

Betty Anne let out a snicker. "Oh my, that's worse than being a saloon girl. We call that place the dirty old man depot."

All three of the girls broke into a fit of giggles. Alannah took a sip of beer while still laughing and choked. Beer shot out of her nose, prompting more giggling.

"I sure hope I did the right thing," Alannah said after regaining her composure.

"Oh, you did. Once you get settled, I bet you'll wonder why you didn't do this years ago," Betty Anne said.

Alannah didn't respond, but sat there quietly. Tears began to well up in her eyes and she rubbed her hand over her mouth. "I know you're right, but one way or the other, in thirty or forty years, I'm going to turn into one of those old shriveled up, sanctimonious biddies that no one can stand. I'll be looking down at young women and treating them as if they're all a bunch of jezebels. It's inevitable. Men might have been put on this earth to drive us crazy, but at least they keep us from turning into dried up old women."

"That's because they like to keep us well-oiled," Wanda said.

The audacious statement caused the girls to break out into another fit of giggles.

Chapter 7

Bozeman, Montana Territory

Eight days had passed since the attack on the Gunther ranch. Ike had recovered enough that he could walk around the house a little with the aid of a cane that Luka had fashioned for him. He remained weak and continued to experience recurring bouts of dizziness from his head injury. Mostly though, he either stayed in bed or sat at the kitchen table and stared through the window at the seven graves.

Ike and Luka had gotten into a heated argument when Ike had insisted on hearing all the details of what had happened to his family. Luka had talked until he was blue in the face to try to convince his brother that no good could come from the information, but had finally given up when Ike had continued haranguing him with the tenacity of a bulldog. The horrors of what had gone on at the ranch had only added to Ike's depression, and he went a full day without speaking.

A knock at the door while the brothers ate lunch caused them to look at each other in surprise.

"This place needs a dog," Luka muttered as he stood.

Luka opened the door to find Sheriff Garr standing there. For an instant, the sight of the sheriff made Luka hopeful that the McClure brothers had been arrested, and then he noticed the telltale signs that bad news was about to be delivered. The sheriff wouldn't make eye contact and his jowly face drooped in defeat.

"May I have a word?" Sheriff Garr asked.

"Certainly. Come on in," Luka replied.

"I'm glad to see that you're up and around," the sheriff said to Ike. "I wasn't too sure that you were going to make it."

"I'm getting a little better each day. What's your news?" Ike asked.

"We tracked those men a good ways past Virginia City and then we lost them. They had extra horses and we were losing ground the farther we went. I'm sorry, but the trail went cold."

"What direction were they going?" Luka asked.

"They stayed in a southwesterly direction."

"They were headed for the Montana Trail," Ike said.

The sheriff glanced down at his feet for a moment before lifting his head to speak. "I'm sure they were, but who knows where they were headed from there. We wouldn't have known where to find them, and there sure would be no tracking them with all the wagons and animals tromping up and down that road."

Luka tended to use his hands when riled. He threw his arms up in the air in exasperation. "They would have headed south. They aren't going to go north and stay in the Montana Territory. You could have asked travelers if they'd seen them. There can't be that many riders with extra horses headed south. Most of the traffic is to the north except for the returning freighters."

"Maybe that's true, but I have a whole county to think about. I couldn't be gone a month chasing down two men," Sheriff Garr replied.

Ike solemnly nodded his head. "Thank you for trying, Sheriff," he said.

"I am going to try to get up some reward money and have posters printed. Maybe a bounty hunter will take an interest in tracking them down. I'm truly sorry I didn't find them, and for your loss."

"I appreciate the offer, but I'd prefer that you didn't print up a poster or offer a reward. If the law can't bring them to justice, I'd just as soon that it be Luka and me. I want to be the one that settles this score," Ike said.

The sheriff frowned and nodded his head. "If that is what you want, then sure, I won't do anything else. Just remember not to get yourselves into trouble, too."

"Sure."

Luka held his tongue and didn't say what he really wanted to say about Sheriff Garr's failure. He escorted the sheriff to the door and thanked him instead. Once the sheriff rode away, he slammed the door and stalked across the room with arms flailing in every direction. "I can't believe he gave up that easily on trying to catch murderers of a woman and children. What is wrong with him?" he raged.

"At least he tried."

"Tried? You're awfully calm in light of the situation. I can't believe you."

Ike took a deep breath that caused him to grimace in pain and exhaled slowly. "To tell you the truth, I expected this. Sheriff Garr is a decent of enough man and sheriff, but he's not cut out for tracking outlaws all over the country. He just isn't."

"God knows where Rusty and Mackey will be by the time you're able to ride."

"We'll find them eventually."

"Well, at least we know what we have to do now. I'm going to go to town and buy me some guns. I've gotten to the point where I'm about as good as I used to be with the rifle, but I have a ways to go with the revolver.

We surely can't share your guns on the trail. I'm also going to try to hire us a foreman and crew to run the ranch while we're gone. We can't let this place go to hell."

"That strikes me as being a sound plan. Luka, I appreciate all you've done and are going to do for me. Not every brother would do this."

"I'm not every brother – I'm your brother."

Ike nodded his head appreciatively. "What about the trading post?"

"I'll just keep having Jeb sell everything out of the back of the wagon until it's gone. We'll worry about rebuilding the store when we get back – whenever that will be."

"I guess I need to get well then."

"That's going to take however long that it takes. We can't get out on the trail and have you get ill. We're going to get them. Don't you worry about that."

"I know."

"I'm going to head out now. I'll see you when I get back."

After Luka had gone, Ike waited another ten minutes to be on the safe side, and then he headed to the barn. He led Nate, his favorite horse, out of the stall and into the hallway. The horse was a tall buckskin, and good-natured. When Ike lifted the saddle onto the gelding's back, he let out a groan and scrunched his face in pain. Undeterred, he managed to bridle and cinch the horse without too much difficulty. Ike grabbed the saddle horn with both hands and took a breath as he steeled himself for what came next. He lifted his foot into the stirrup and swung his leg up over the horse. The effort caused him to catch his breath from a stabbing pain in his chest as if he'd been knifed. He also felt lightheaded so he sucked in air in hopes of warding off the condition. A good minute passed, but the pain and dizziness disappeared. After a lifetime of being healthy as a horse, recovering from his injuries had already gotten way past being old. He pressed Nate's sides and the horse walked out of the barn.

"Good boy," Ike praised. "This isn't so bad once I'm in the saddle."

For the next fifteen minutes, Ike rode the horse at a walk around the yard. The accomplishment brought a smile to his face. For the first time since getting shot, he actually felt a little hopeful that life would go on in some fashion or other.

"Let's try to go a little faster," Ike said as he pressed the ribs of the horse.

Nate moved out into a trot. The horse hadn't covered thirty feet at the new gait before the jarring sent so much pain coursing through Ike's chest that he hollered and yanked back the reins. The bouncing also caused a bad case of vertigo. Ike's head was swimming. He reached out to grab the saddle horn for balance, but his perception was so off that he missed. As Nate abruptly stopped, Ike's momentum shifted forward and he fell out of the saddle. He bounced on the ground and let out a groan before flopping onto his back and closing his eyes. He rolled his head in the dirt for a moment, trying to clear his head, and lost consciousness.

Luka, after three hours in town, rode toward the ranch trying to get used to the feeling of having a holstered gun strapped around his waist again after so long a time. During his days in the war and as a deputy, he had felt naked not wearing one, but now the weapon felt foreign and obtrusive. He kept glancing down at the new rifle in its scabbard as he slowly came to terms with the fact that he might once again have to kill another human being. When he'd opened the trading post, he really thought those days were behind him and he really wished it had stayed that way.

As Luka neared the ranch, he spotted Nate standing in the yard. The sight was at first puzzling and then a feeling of dread washed over him. He spurred his horse into a gallop and raced toward the house. In the distance, he saw Ike crawling around in the yard trying to get to his feet. Luka reined in his horse and jumped from the saddle before the animal came to a stop.

"What in the hell are you doing? Are you trying to kill yourself?" Luka yelled as he ran toward his brother.

Ike collapsed onto his back. Blood had seeped through his shirt where the bullet wounds had reopened and he was soaked in sweat. His breathing sounded like a dog panting and he labored to speak. "Thought I could ride," he whispered.

"Damn it, Ike, you know you aren't ready. You can barely walk around the house. The only thing you've done is set us back at least a week. Let's get you inside and doctored up." Luka bent down to grab his brother's arm.

Ike shot his arm up with his palm out to signal Luka to stop. "Luka, promise me you'll kill Rusty and Mackey. Please do that for me. I'm going to stay here until I die. I just want to be with Irene and the kids." Tears brimmed over his lower eyelids and mixed in with the dust on his cheeks.

The pleading expression on Ike's face unnerved Luka. He dropped onto his butt and placed his hand on Ike's leg. A misty feeling came over him that he tried to fight off, but tears ran down his cheeks, too. "Ike, you know Irene would not want this. You're a fighter and she'd expect you to fight. We're Gunthers and we don't quit. It's just not in our nature. I miss your family, too, but this is just a setback is all it is. You'll be mad at yourself in the morning if you're dead."

The ridiculous statement brought Ike out of his grieving long enough to give a little chuckle. "That's a pretty damn silly thing to say."

"Not as silly as what you said," Luka retorted.

Ike held out his arm. "Get me inside and douse me with that medicine. I surely don't want to die from my wounds getting all full of pus."

With Luka's support, Ike made it to the house and into bed. Luka examined the wounds and treated them with carbolic acid before applying fresh bandages.

"It's not as bad as I feared. Looks like you just pulled the scabs loose. I think you'll live," Luka pronounced.

"I guess I won't get to be mad at myself in the morning after all," Ike joked.

Luka smiled and nodded his head. "I do have some good news. I hired Dalton Schultz away from the Barber ranch to be our foreman. Had to pay him fifty dollars a month to do it, but whenever he's been in the trading post, he always struck me as a cut above most of these cowboys. He says he knows just who to hire for our hands, too. It'll save me the trouble."

"Thank you, Luka. I don't know what I'd do without you."

"Same goes for me. You get some rest now. I have me some new guns to break in. I think I'll be needing them."

Chapter 8

Montana Trail, Montana Territory

The McClure brothers were in bad moods and barely speaking to each other. After buying the supplies from the old codger, they had ridden for three days in hopes of advancing upon a returning southbound freighter. Their efforts had been for naught, and both men were tired and sore from all the riding. Rusty had wanted to rob every lone settler along the way, but Mackey had refused. The brothers had nearly come to blows over the matter, but Mackey got his way. They were nearing the part of the trail where it flattened into easier travel for a stretch that ran clear past Pocatello Junction. An attack on the freighters would be dangerous out in open terrain so they made camp in the mountains to wait for their prey. Three more days passed with no sighting of a returning freighter.

The two men were sitting in their camp while sharing a can of cold beans. An argument over whose turn it was to go gather firewood had led to an impasse. Instead, they did without a fire or warm food. The day felt blazing hot anyway, and Mackey figured a fire would have only added to the temperature and their ill moods.

"If I have to look at your face for one more minute, I might just take my knife out and cut it off," Rusty groused.

"Yeah, you try that whenever you're ready. You'll be leaking water every time you take a drink if you do," Mackey replied.

Mackey's bravado caused Rusty to laugh. "We need us a diversion. If we get rich robbing a freighter, I just might use my half of the money on a woman. I could sure use one about now."

"I hear that. I could use one, too. We have six years of prison life to make up for."

"Well, Ike Gunther won't be sending us back there – that's for sure. It still grieves me that we didn't get Luka though."

"We can't do anything about it now," Mackey said.

"Do you ever wonder if we would have turned out differently if we'd had a pa like Ike and Luka? I'm not blaming Ma or anything, but we were too wild for her to tame."

"I never thought about being like the Gunthers, but sure, I've wondered what life would have been like with a pa. We didn't have no choice but to be mean to survive."

"True, but I think it just came natural to us."

Mackey gave a small chuckle. "Probably. You know, Rusty, we could still go straight if you're having second thoughts. It's not too late."

"Sure it is. After what we did to Ike and his family, we're condemned to hell as sure as I'm sitting here. We should have had this talk before then if we wanted a different life. I say we take whatever we want and do as we please from here on out."

"Better days are ahead," Mackey said as he stood and used his spyglass to study the trail to the north. "In fact, maybe it's today. There's a mule train coming this way."

Rusty jumped up and grabbed his Winchester. "You run across the trail and take your position. When I shoot the driver, you shoot the lead mules. We'll have them then."

"Just make sure you don't miss." Mackey retrieved his rifle and saddlebag filled with cartridges.

"I'm not going to miss. Hurry up."

Mackey scrambled down the slope and across the trail into a rock formation where he could take cover.

An excruciating ten minutes passed before the freighter neared the brothers. Rusty waited until the mule train was as close as possible while still being able to get a frontal shot on the driver. He took aim at the man's heart and gently squeezed the trigger. The roar of the gun brought an end to the sleepy quiet of the afternoon. As the driver grabbed his chest, he tilted forward and plunged between the wagon and the last team of mules.

Mackey quickly fired two shots that knocked down the lead team of mules and brought the wagon to a standstill.

The bullwhackers were running around and twisting their heads in every direction, confused as to the location of the shooters. Rusty, taking advantage of the mayhem, put a bead on one of the men and fired his rifle. The bullwhacker took off in a sprint and ran seven steps before dropping dead.

The remaining men were spurred into action at the sight of their second companion falling dead. Two of the bullwhackers dove underneath the first wagon to take cover while the third man crawled under the belly of a mule and positioned himself between a pair of the animals. The bullwhackers began returning fire. From their many years of freighting, the men were seasoned in fighting and survival. Their barrage of gunfire made it nearly impossible for the McClures to get off clean shots.

Rusty stretched his body up just enough above his hiding spot to take a shot, but before he could fire, a bullet ricocheted off the rock near him. Gravel smacked into his face, and he let out a scream that his brother could hear clear from his hiding spot. Rusty flopped back onto the ground and rolled around in intense pain. His face felt as if it was on fire where the rocks had imbedded into his flesh. For a moment, he thought he might die until he took stock of the situation and realized the nature of his injuries.

"Rusty, Rusty, are you alive?" Mackey kept bellowing.

"I'm fine. Just get these sons of bitches killed," Rusty finally yelled to shut up his brother.

Rusty was incensed by his injuries. He took aim at the two mules providing cover for the one bullwhacker. His shots maimed the animals and they thrashed around wildly to escape their harnesses. The bushwhacker was getting stepped on and crushed between the two mules. In an act of desperation, he tried to make an escape, only to get entangled in the harnesses. As he frantically worked to free his legs, Mackey put a bullet in his head. The man dropped to the ground like a quail shot from the air.

The gunfight continued with the remaining two bullwhackers. Rusty hit one of the men in the kneecap. The injury caused the man to roll around under the wagon while screaming nonstop. The shrieks of agony were unnerving for everyone, especially his partner. While the remaining bullwhacker valiantly held the McClures at bay, he ran out of cartridges. The brothers realized what was happening and waited for the man to make a run for more ammunition. He bolted on Mackey's side and raced toward the last wagon. A shot to the back felled him as he neared his destination. All the while, the surviving bushwhacker continued screaming in agony. Rusty set his rifle against the rocks and jogged down to the wagon to put an end to the noise.

"Shut the hell up," Rusty hollered. He drew his revolver and calmly kept shooting the bullwhacker until he was indeed silenced.

Mackey found the last man he had shot attempting to crawl away into the brush. The bullwhacker heard Mackey running toward him and rolled onto his back.

"Mister, take what you want and please just leave me be. I promise not to give the law your description if you let me live. I have a family," the man pleaded.

The begging gave Mackey pause. He didn't want to shoot the man again. The bullwhacker didn't look that much different from him or Rusty, and the only purpose killing him would serve was to protect them from identification. Rusty, on the other hand, would never allow such a loose end. Mackey slowly pulled his Colt from the holster. "I wish I could let you live," he said before putting a bullet in the bullwhacker's head.

"Let's find the money and get the hell out of here. We made enough ruckus to raise the dead," Rusty yelled.

Mackey glanced over his shoulder at his brother and did a double take. Rusty's face looked a bloody mess with punctures to his cheeks and forehead.

"You're supposed to duck before they shoot," Mackey said.

"Screw you. I could have lost an eye. Just remember that whichever one of them did this – well, he's dead."

The brothers began rummaging through the wagons. In the rear cart, Mackey finally found a lockbox stashed under a pile of tarps. He dragged the box out and tossed it onto the ground. "I found it," he hollered.

Rusty came strutting up with his revolver drawn. "I'll open it," he said.

The shot hit the padlock and sent a piece of metal flying through the air, catching Rusty on the shinbone just above his boot. He let out a yelp and started dancing a one-legged jig.

Mackey covered his mouth with his hand in an attempt to suppress a laugh, but the sight of his brother was just too funny to hold in. When he finally stopped giggling, he said, "You won't have to worry about spending that money on a woman. You can't dance no more and you're all scarred up. No woman would have you," he said.

"Ma wouldn't be any the wiser if I shot you right here on the spot. Go get me a rifle and shut your mouth."

After Mackey returned with a Winchester, Rusty snatched it from his hands and stepped off a good distance before taking aim at the box. Three more shots tore into the padlock before it disintegrated.

Mackey raced his hobbled brother to the treasure and beat him. Inside the box, he found two large leather pouches that he yanked out and held up into the air as if he'd won prizes. "They're heavy," he shouted with a crazed grin.

"Take a quick peek inside, and then we got to go."

Mackey handed one of the bags to Rusty. The brothers opened the pouches and dumped an assortment of gold coins into their palms.

"We're rich," Mackey announced.

As Rusty returned the coins back into the bag, he said, "We need to cover some ground. When the freighter company finds out about this, they'll be sending a posse to recover this much money – maybe even the Pinkertons."

"Just think what we can buy Ma with all of this," Mackey mused. He staggered a little as he walked away as if drunk on his newfound wealth.

Chapter 9

Pocatello Junction, Idaho Territory

Rusty and Mackey rode hard for the next three days to put as much distance as possible between them and the carnage they'd left behind on the freighter. The brothers made a point of avoiding coming face-to-face with other travelers on the trail so that nobody got a good look at them. On the third night, they made camp a few miles from Pocatello Junction. The brothers were tired from all of the riding and hungry for a decent meal after having lived on beans and jerky for days. A failed attempt to find a rabbit to shoot forced them to eat the same meal again. They crawled into their bedrolls before the sky had even turned completely dark.

Before riding into the village the next morning, Rusty insisted they hide their newfound wealth. After searching for the perfect spot, he found a place to his liking in a grove of cottonwoods near the river to bury the gold coins. Satisfied the loot was safe, the brothers headed toward civilization.

Pocatello Junction wasn't much for the eye to see. The place served as a trading center for miners and settlers, and appeared short on luxuries. Most of the buildings looked as though they'd been thrown up with whatever scrap lumber was available. Two saloons, a few trading posts, and two restaurants made up most of the village. A one-room building, filled with cots, functioned as a lodging house for travelers.

"This is more like a one-pony town than a one-horse one," Rusty scoffed as they rode down the street.

"As long as they've got food and beer, I don't give a hoot. You be on your best behavior. We don't need to bring attention to ourselves," Mackey lectured.

Rusty gave his brother a brisk little salute. "Yes, sir. And you make sure you don't call out my name. We need to make sure we leave here without anybody knowing who we are."

Mackey nodded his head with a touch of condescension. "Let's eat."

The brothers walked into a little restaurant. The place had four tables and more flies than a cattle lot. A scrawny old lady served as waitress, cook, and proprietor. She took their orders without comment before disappearing to go cook the meals. When she returned, she carried two plates that were heaped with ham, bacon, eggs, and biscuits. Mackey was notorious for his sweet tooth and drowned his plate in syrup.

"You should just buy syrup and pour it on dirt. You can't possibly taste anything but that sweet stuff. It would save us some money," Rusty said.

"Oh, shut up. I don't fault you for what you eat. You're the one that likes Rocky Mountain oysters. I wouldn't put those things in my mouth even if I was starving to death. I've never called you out for eating them."

"You just did."

Mackey shook his head. "Only because you did first. Just eat."

They ate the rest of their breakfasts without speaking another word. When they finished, Rusty paid the bill that the old lady had left on the table. She took the money without having said another word since asking what they wanted to eat.

The brothers walked to a trading post and bought all the supplies they could manage to stuff into their saddlebags. Their four horses were looking a little ragged from all the travel so they took them to the livery stable and paid the blacksmith to reshoe all the animals and to give them extra grain. Afterward, they checked out the two saloons and were disappointed to find them empty of customers with whom to strike up a card game. With nothing else to do, Rusty and Mackey sauntered over to the boarding house to rest. Rusty blanched at the two-dollar-a-cot price, but when the proprietor told him he could always find a shady tree to sleep under, the brothers forked over the money and went to bed.

Mackey woke up hungry in the late afternoon. He roused Rusty, and received a good cussing for his effort. They decided to try the other restaurant in hopes of a more congenial reception. The place had several men in it, all busy shoving food into their faces. A cute waitress with a big smile, black hair, and a curvy body came over to the table and started making eyes at and flirting with Mackey while taking their orders. The exchange didn't go unnoticed by Rusty. He crossed his arms and sulked as they waited for their meals.

"Why'd she flirt with you and not me?" Rusty asked in a sulky voice.

"Because I'm the good-looking one in the family and your face has so many scabs on it that you look as if you have smallpox. Women don't like that red hair either," Mackey replied with a devilish grin.

"I don't have red hair. Ma always called it strawberry blond."

"Call it what you want. One way or the other, it's a girl's color."

"Oh, screw you."

When the waitress returned a short while later with beefsteaks, baked potatoes, and beans, she set the food on the table and then suggestively thrust her butt out and placed her hand on her hip. "Is there anything else I can get you?" she asked with a smile.

Rusty scowled. "We're fine. You can get out of here and leave us be is what you can do," he barked.

The waitress frowned and made a quick retreat.

"You're pathetic," Mackey said. "I wouldn't begrudge you a little female companionship if the tables were turned."

"You aren't me, are you? Just eat and spare me the sermon."

The brothers continued bickering throughout the rest of the meal. By the time they finished eating, they were nearly ready to come to blows. After they paid the tab, they stormed out of the restaurant toward the nearest saloon.

The Pocatello Saloon was a dark and dirty establishment. Between the poor lighting and smoke, everything looked gray. The floor appeared as if it hadn't been swept in years, and all the spilt beer caused the brothers' boots to stick to the boards as they walked across the room. The saloon was now filled with miners and locals, causing Rusty and Mackey to have to force their way up to the bar. They both ordered a beer, and then Rusty headed for the poker tables. Mackey didn't like playing cards and was content to stand at the bar and enjoy his first beer in what seemed like a lifetime.

As the evening wore on and darkness fell, Mackey continued standing at the bar, drinking one beer after another. He couldn't get the waitress out of his mind and contemplated heading back to the restaurant to see if she might be near to finishing her shift. Her flirtations combined with the alcohol had made him lusty. He was also getting bored. No one would ever accuse the inhabitants of Pocatello Junction of being overly social to strangers.

Meanwhile, Rusty was having to the time of his life. He was on a winning streak like he'd never before seen. It seemed as if he could do no wrong with how he played his cards. Each time he raked the money his way, his laughter and boisterous bragging would cut through the din of the crowd while his opponents grew increasingly agitated.

When Rusty won another hand with three aces, a miner that had bet his last dollar on two pair became enraged.

"You're nothing but a card cheat. Nobody can win that many hands unless they're cheating," the man shouted.

"Whoa there, I don't need to cheat. Lady Luck has been smiling down on me, and to be honest, you're not much of a card player," Rusty replied.

The exchange of words had caught the crowd's attention, and they had grown quiet as they watched the argument. Fearing trouble was about to unfold, Mackey eased his way toward the card table.

"You just took a whole week of my pay and I want it back," the miner demanded.

"Mister, you shouldn't be playing cards if you are not willing to lose your stake. I did not cheat you. Now you best be on your way before you rile me up good," Rusty warned, his tone even but forceful.

"I said it once and I'll say it again, you ain't nothing but a damn card cheat." The miner jumped up from his seat and fumbled for the gun that he kept tucked in his pants.

Rusty hadn't expected such a rash move and was caught unprepared for the attack. The dirty floor caused him to struggle to slide his chair back to get to his gun. When the miner finally freed his revolver from his trousers, Rusty's eyes got as big as silver dollars. He watched helplessly as the gun barrel was leveled at him. Before the miner managed to cock his gun, Mackey drew his Colt and shot the miner in the back.

"Let's get the hell out of here," Mackey yelled.

With a flip of the table, Rusty freed himself. He and Mackey ran for the door, firing their guns above the heads of the patrons as they did so. As the customers dove to the floor for safety, the brothers nearly tripped over the bodies sprawled around the room.

"I had to leave all that money," Rusty complained as they made it into the street.

"But you got to keep your life."

"Maybe. We ain't out of here yet."

The brothers ran into the livery stable. In the dark barn, they fumbled to find a lantern. Their blundering roused the blacksmith, and he walked out of the room he slept in to see what was going on.

Rusty pointed his revolver at the man. "Get all of our horses saddled, and make it quick if you want to live," he hollered.

The blacksmith lit a lantern and leered at the brothers before scurrying toward a stall. "I knew you boys were trouble as soon as I laid eyes upon you," he muttered.

While peeking out the barn door, Mackey said, "There's a crowd gathering, but at least this town doesn't have a lawman. That might save us."

Rusty marched to the door. "If you want to ever see your blacksmith alive again, you better hold your fire. One shot and he's a dead man," he bellowed.

The warning gave the crowd pause and caused indecision in the ranks. In the lull, Mackey helped get the horses saddled while Rusty remained on watch.

"We're ready," Mackey announced.

Rusty pulled a gold double eagle twenty-dollar piece from his pocket and tossed it at the blacksmith. "Much obliged for taking care of our horses. Now I want you to let all the other horses out of their stalls. When I give the word, I want you to open the barn doors."

The blacksmith rubbed the coin between his thumb and fingers. "That's going to piss off a lot of people," he said.

"Better than being dead."

With a nod of his head, the blacksmith headed for a stall. He began opening stall doors and pulling horses into the barn's hallway. When he had the dozen horses freed, he walked to the end of the barn and looked toward Rusty.

"Let them fly," Rusty hollered.

The blacksmith threw open the doors. The brothers fired their revolvers and spurred their mounts. All of the freed horses bolted for the door and sent the crowd standing outside scurrying for safety. The brothers made their escape without a single shot being fired at them. A few of the men that had horses tied at the saloons gave chase, but soon gave up in the dark night to return to town.

Rusty and Mackey made it back to the cottonwoods. With no moonlight, they had to search for their loot with matches. Rusty was cussing up a storm and running around like a chicken with its head cut off by the time that Mackey found the right spot. They dug up their treasure like two dogs racing for a buried bone.

"What now?" Mackey asked.

"We need to head east and get off this trail. In a day or two, word is going to reach this way about the freighter we robbed. They'll be suspecting that it was us after this night, and I want to be long gone."

"So much for getting some rest."

"I know. It's going to be a long night. At least we got plenty of sleep today."

The brothers mounted up and began trying to find their way in the pitch-black night.

"So were you cheating?" Mackey asked.

"No, not at all. It grieves me to think of all that money I left on that floor. I couldn't do no wrong. That was the luckiest night of cards I've ever played."

"Well, I think your luck done ran out."

Chapter 10

Nevada City, Colorado

As Alannah changed into a fresh dress after a day of working at the store, she already dreaded her evening. Her sister, Carol, was having a birthday party for her daughter, Chloe. This would be the first family function held since Alannah had moved out on her own. With a family as big as hers, somebody was always having a birthday, and when they all got together, moving about proved nearly impossible without bumping into somebody. And to top things off, her parents were still barely speaking to her, and she knew one of her sisters would have something pithy to say about her leaving home.

Alannah was the last to arrive at Carol's home. The front room was stuffed with family members and she had to weave her way through the crowd to add her gift to the stack already on the table.

"Happy Birthday, Chloe," Alannah called out.

The newly turned five-year-old held up her hand and waved. She and Alannah had bonded from the first time that Alannah had held her in her arms as an infant. Chloe grinned at her aunt and then disappeared in pursuit of one of her cousins.

Alannah began making the rounds to speak to everyone. Her mother and father greeted her stiffly, making sure that all the family could see for their own eyes their disapproval of her actions. Alannah put on a brave face and acted as if nothing was out of the ordinary. When she got to her sister, Nellie, she could see from the smug expression that trouble was about ready to brew.

"So I hear you've moved into old Miss Ryan's home," Nellie said.

"I did. I decided I'd reached a point in my life where I should try being on my own. The only thing I've ever known is living at home," Alannah replied.

"You must think you're quite the independent woman these days." Nellie's tone dripped with sarcasm.

"If you mean that I'm not saddled with three kids and a husband to take care of, then yes, I'm quite independent."

Nellie bristled at the comment and gave her sister a hard look. "I guess it makes it more convenient for all your gentlemen callers."

"It sure does. I just hang a red lantern in the window and they come a flocking like a herd of sheep."

With a snicker, Nellie said, "That's a good one. We all know the truth about you and men these days. You have certainly moved into the right house. I doubt a man has set foot inside that place in the last fifty years. I'm sure the trend will continue."

The cruelty of Nellie's words caught Alannah off guard. She could feel her face turning red and she fought the urge to burst into tears. "I hope that made you feel good about yourself." Alannah pushed her way through her relatives and went outside to sit down on the swing. She sucked in a loud breath, determined not to cry.

A couple of minutes later, the door opened and Carol came outside.

"Carol, don't you dare start with me. I've already had my fill with Nellie," Alannah warned.

Carol waved her hand through the air to signal she wasn't there for trouble. She took a seat beside Alannah on the swing. "Don't let Nellie get the best of you. You know how she can be," she said.

"Why would she say something so mean? She was looking for trouble from the moment she first spoke to me," Alannah whined.

"Nellie is always going to try to curry favor with Daddy and Momma – that's just the way she is. They've certainly made it clear how they feel about you moving out of their home. I don't think Nellie can really help herself. She'll get to feeling guilty in a couple of days and come apologize to you. You know she will. She's done it her whole life."

"I suppose, but it doesn't make it any better right now. It hurts to know that not only does the whole town think I'm a hopeless old maid, but my family does too."

Carol patted Alannah's leg. "I don't think that and I'm proud of you for moving out. You gave up Luka for Daddy and Momma. You should at least get to have a life of your own. You've sacrificed enough."

"Do you really mean that?" Alannah's voice sounded childlike.

"Yes, I do."

"I've never gotten over Luka and I suspect I never will. Sometimes, I think I made a mistake letting him go."

"You're not going to like hearing this, but I think you did, too. I always thought you should have just up and eloped with Luka. The family would have come around to the marriage eventually."

"Really? Why in darnation didn't you say something before now?"

"Because it wasn't my place. If you had decided to elope with him, it should have been a decision that you came to all by yourself. Nobody should have had a say in that but you and Luka."

"I think you've managed to make me feel worse than Nellie did."

Carol smiled and again patted Alannah's leg. "Nellie tried to be mean, I'm just being honest. That's a big difference. Now we need to get back inside and celebrate Chloe's birthday. You know you're her favorite aunt. She'd be crushed if you went home without eating some cake and singing to her."

"Thanks for the talk, Carol. I needed to hear that somebody is on my side. You'd better keep Nellie away from me though or I'm liable to yank every hair out of her head and shove them down her throat."

Carol got tickled. "We certainly wouldn't want any drama in the O'Sullivan family, now would we?"

Chapter 11

Bozeman, Montana Territory

Ike Gunther's fall from the horse wasn't as bad of a setback as first feared. He had spent a couple of days bedridden before his aches and pains subsided enough to allow him to resume walking. When he took his first few steps, he was relieved to find his dizziness had vanished. He tossed the cane in the corner of the bedroom, determined to get well.

For the next week, Ike pushed himself to take a daily walk that grew a little longer each day. In his better moments, he began to believe he would make a full recovery. His appetite returned with a vengeance, and he ate seconds at every meal in the hopes of regaining his strength as rapidly as possible.

Every time Ike walked out the front door, the sight of the seven graves off to the side of the yard would catch him off guard. He'd catch his breath every time. His stomach would feel like it was coming up into his throat and his pulse would quicken. He secretly wished that Luka had picked a spot behind the house so that the cemetery wasn't such a constant reminder of all he'd lost. On most days, his grief made him feel so hollow that he thought he just might collapse into a pile of skin and bones. Whenever the thoughts of Irene and the children became too much to bear, he banished them from his mind with vows to find and kill Rusty and Mackey McClure. Vengeance remained the driving force in his recovery.

As noon neared, Ike stood at the stove, keeping an eye on the slabs of steak he was frying in a skillet. His belly growled and the smell of the cooking meat had his mouth watering. The sound of the front door closing caused him to look over his shoulder to see that Luka had returned from his trip to town. With a grin, he said, "I decided I'd had about all of your cooking I could stand. If I'm ever going to get well, I need me a decently cooked meal. Steaks shouldn't chew like shoe leather."

"I'll remember to let you fend for yourself the next time I find you near dead," Luka replied. He smiled begrudgingly. The sight of Ike acting like his old self filled him with some hope that better days lay ahead. He also couldn't help but notice that his brother had bathed, shaved, and combed his hair. "Nice to see you found your razor."

"Yeah, I was getting to where I couldn't stand myself. I was getting a little on the rank side."

"I hoped that you might notice," Luka said drolly.

"The steaks will be done by the time you get the table set."

"You must be feeling better. You're back to being your naturally bossy self."

Luka retrieved the plates and silverware while Ike brought the steaks and baked potatoes to the table. The hungry brothers wasted no time in taking their seats and attacking their meals.

"Since you proclaim to be a better cook than me, I guess you can do all the cooking when we hit the trail," Luka said.

Ike grinned. "Well played," he said.

"Now, on to a discussion of business. Jeb has sold most of the merchandise out of the wagon. I told him he could have the rest of it to sell for himself. We made our money back and then some. Jeb has been a good employee and he's going to be out of work now."

"Fine by me. I hope we can get him to return to work for us whenever we get around to opening the trading post back up."

"Dalton is working out just fine as the ranch foreman. He seems to have put a good crew together, and he sure works them."

"I've noticed on my walks. That man seems to be a perfectionist. He's already fixed those couple of loose boards on the stalls that I've been putting off forever. He's liable to put me out of a job. I guess I can sit at my desk and be a ranch baron," Ike said.

"That would suit you just fine. You never liked to get your hands dirty anyway."

"I would talk. If my memory serves me well, you were the one that took the trading post position."

Luka shook his head in dismay. "Let's just change the subject because our memories seem to be different on the reasons for our decisions on who did what."

Ike smiled. "Nah, I just had to say something in my defense. Hurry up and eat your steak. We're going to go for a horse ride afterward."

"Ike, I don't think that's a good idea. You need to wait a few more days."

"I'm not going to do anything silly like I did last time. I just want to see how I feel now. You'll be right there with me if I get into trouble."

With a sigh of resignation, and against his better judgment, Luka nodded his head. "All right then, but you better keep your word."

The brothers walked to the barn, and while Ike put on the bridles, Luka saddled the horses. They headed at an easy walk in the direction of the cattle herd.

"How's it feel?" Luka asked.

"Better than last time – that's for sure. For better or worse, my head feels back to normal."

"How about your chest?"

"Well, let's just say that I know I've been shot, but it's manageable."

When the men neared the herd, they pulled their horses to a stop and gazed out over the cattle.

"The herd looks good. You've done a fine job of building it up since we first started," Luka said.

Ike let out a snort. "I guess me about dying has made you turn over a new leaf. Since when did you begin handing out compliments?"

"Maybe it has, but it's the truth. I just wanted to let you know. And for the record, I've always sung your praises way more than you ever have mine."

With a wry smile, Ike looked over at his brother. "I guess about dying has changed me, too. You're absolutely right about that. You did a fine job with the trading post. The ranch would have never survived without you winning over the townsfolk and miners to do business at our store. That money saved us."

Luka slowly nodded his head for a moment before speaking. "And we both owe the idea to Irene," he said.

The remark caused Ike to grimace in an expression of profound loss. Only a man that had lost everything could show such pain. His eyes looked like dying embers and the creases in his face made him look old beyond his years. He spun Nate around and spurred the horse into a lope in the direction of the house.

"Damn it, Ike, you promised," Luka hollered before giving chase.

Nate was a fast horse with long strides, and Luka had no chance of catching his brother without putting his own horse into a full-out gallop. He resisted the urge to do so for fear that Ike would do the same.

Ike made it to the house and stopped in front of the barn. He gave Luka a grin when his brother rode up and yanked his gelding to a halt. "About time you got here," he said.

"Don't you dare grin at me. You gave me your word. If you tear those wounds open, we'll never get to go after Rusty and Mackey," Luka fumed.

"I said I wouldn't do anything silly, and I didn't do that. I knew what I was doing. I'm ready to ride. We'll leave in the morning."

"You know darn well that we won't be doing much loping. We'll be spending hours a day at a trot. I seriously doubt you're strong enough to post in the saddle for long stretches at a time, and you won't be able to stand the jarring."

"I'm healed up. That's all that matters. I'll just have to buck up and take it. We're leaving in the morning – end of discussion."

"This discussion will be over when I say it is. You are not ready to ride. We can't be in the middle of nowhere and have you go down. Give it one more week."

"Luka, the McClures are liable to be clear to Texas if we don't get on the trail. I promise you that I can ride. I've lost everything I've ever cared about except for you. Rusty and Mackey are going to regret they ever knew me. I'm leaving in the morning with or without you."

Luka gave Ike an icy stare before jumping off his horse and grabbing the reins to lead the animal into the barn. "Fine, but you can unsaddle your own damn horse if you're all that well. I need to get some more practicing in with my revolver."

Chapter 12

Southwest Montana Territory

In the first light of early morning, Ike and Luka headed out in their pursuit of the McClure brothers. They brought a packhorse with them that they had loaded with enough provisions to go weeks without having to worry about resupplying.

Ike glanced over his shoulder one last time at his house and the graves of his family. He had a feeling it would be a long time before he saw them again.

After they had ridden a couple of miles from the house, Luka put his horse into a brisk trot. He figured he'd find out real quick whether Ike was up to the challenge of riding before they got out in the middle of nowhere. Ike's insistence that they leave today still riled him to no end. Luka knew his brother wasn't ready for the long ride that stretched before them.

Ike showed no emotion when Luka sped up the pace. He pressed his mount into a trot and began posting to the rhythm of the horse's gait. His legs felt a little weak and the jarring caused pain to shoot through his chest, but come hell or high water, he decided he would die in the saddle before complaining.

"How are you holding up?" Luka asked after they had ridden a couple of miles.

Ike looked over at his brother and forced a smile. "I'm just fine. You just worry about yourself. I can outride you any day of the week."

"I'm not worried about any day. I'm worried about today. How do you really feel?"

"It might take a day or two to get my legs back under me, and if I'm being honest, my chest hurts some, but it's manageable. We have a job to do."

"You're a tough old cuss," Luka said admiringly.

"And don't you forget it. I can still kick your ass whenever I want."

Luka let out a chuckle. "That knock you took to the head didn't damage your high opinion of yourself either."

The brothers continued riding to the west. The morning had started with a chill in the air, but by ten o'clock, they had removed their jackets, and by noon, their shirts were soaked in sweat. They spent most of their time alternating their horses' gaits between a walk and a trot, occasionally breaking into a lope to make some good time. The pace wore Ike down though he never complained and tried not to show his discomfort. His legs felt like they had turned to jelly and his chest hurt and was getting sore. He secretly worried that he might not be able to ride the following day.

About the only time Luka rode horseback anymore was when he went back and forth between the ranch and town. His legs were burning, and he worried that the trip had to be even worse for Ike. In spite of the circumstances, he enjoyed being on the trail again with his brother. A long time had passed since they had traveled together. It seemed like old times as long as he didn't ponder on the reason for their mission.

The landscape eventually changed from flatlands rich in thick green grass and dotted with cattle into foothills. Even then, the countryside looked sufficient for grazing, and would make for good ranching if somebody was willing to live so far from a town. To Ike's relief, the trail still made for easy and fast travel as it weaved around the hills.

In the early afternoon, they reached the point where they needed to turn south in their journey toward Virginia City. To the north, two riders could be seen headed their way at a distance of a quarter of a mile or better.

"Wonder where they're headed?" Luka asked.

"Don't know, but I've never cared for having someone at my rear. Makes us too easy of a target. When we get around that bend, let's stop and wait for them. I could use a break anyway, and we'll see how they act," Ike replied.

The trail curved around a foothill, and when the brothers had ridden around the rise and were out of sight of the riders, they came to a stop. Ike climbed off his horse and had to hang on to the saddle horn when his legs wanted to buckle. He stood there a moment until able to stiffly shuffle over to a rock and take a seat. As he took a deep breath, he removed the thong from the hammer of his Colt.

"Did you ever get to where you could shoot a revolver again?" Ike asked.

"Finally, I did. I might have spent most of our savings on cartridges to do it though," Luka said with a snort. "I thought I was never going to get back to the point where I could hit anything on the draw, but it eventually came back to me."

"Good. Just be ready. These men might be harmless, but it never hurts to be cautious."

Luka rolled his eyes. Sometimes his brother proved insufferable. He would have reminded Ike who had been in charge during the war, but he wasn't in the mood to rehash that debate for the thousandth time.

As the two strangers rounded the bend, their expressions failed to conceal their surprise at finding Ike and Luka waiting for them. The men looked to be in their early twenties. Both were freshly shaved and barbered. Their clothing was what ranch hands would wear, and the newness of the outfits suggested they hadn't been on the trail for a long period of time.

"Howdy," one of the men called out.

"Hello," Ike greeted. "We're taking us a little rest. It's been a while since we spent the day in the saddle."

"I can understand that. These saddles don't get any softer as the day goes on. My name is Seth and this here is Leo."

The men got down from their horses and walked over to shake hands.

"I'm Ike Gunther and this is my brother, Luka."

After all of them had exchanged handshakes, Seth asked, "So where are you headed to?"

"We're headed for the Montana Trail. We have business to the south. How about you?" Luka responded.

"We are on our way to Virginia City. We're gamblers, and we figure we'll take some money off those miners' hands," Seth answered with a confident grin.

Luka nodded his head. He didn't believe Seth for a minute. Gamblers were an independent lot and didn't tend to travel in pairs. And besides that, he had noticed when they shook hands that both men's palms were calloused and rough. Gamblers had hands as soft as a baby's butt.

"That's a dangerous line of work," Ike said.

For the first time, Leo seemed to take heed of the conversation. He pulled his shoulders back and frowned. "We don't cheat at cards. There's no danger if you play fair," he said, his voice defensive.

Seth gave Leo a dirty look before turning his attention back to Ike and Luka. "Leo is a bit sensitive about his honesty and sometimes takes things out of context. Don't mind him."

"We're all good," Ike said. He stared at Leo to see if the young man had anything else he wanted to say.

"I didn't mean nothing," Leo offered.

"Nothing taken from it," Ike responded.

Seth seemed anxious to change the subject. He popped his hands against his thighs and gave a friendly smile. "Since we're all headed in the same direction, how do you feel about making camp together? We have our own food and we'd be happy to share a meal together. Some new company is nice now and then."

Ike paused a moment before answering. He had no desire to make camp with the men, but quickly decided that it would be best to keep them close at hand rather than have to worry about where they could be lurking farther up the trail. "Well, sure. We don't mind at all. Let's ride," he said.

Luka didn't like the situation one bit. He didn't trust these men any farther than he could throw them. Something about them just wasn't quite right and he wondered if Ike felt so tired that he missed it. He glanced at his brother and received a wink that informed him that Ike was on the same page as he was.

The men mounted up and resumed the ride toward Virginia City. Seth was inquisitive and peppered Ike and Luka with questions. The men willingly answered the inquiries without mentioning the tragedy that had befallen the family. Seth and Leo, on the other hand, were less than forthright when responding to questions about their pasts. They were from Texas, though where in Texas was not revealed. As for what jobs they'd worked at in the past, Seth said only that they'd done a little of everything before turning to gambling.

Late in the day, they came upon a creek and decided to make camp for the night. Ike estimated they were about fifteen miles from Virginia City. He took charge of the camp and sent Seth and Leo off to gather firewood while he and Luka retrieved cooking gear and food from the packhorse.

"What do you make of those two?" Luka asked.

Ike looked over his shoulder to make sure Seth and Leo were out of sight. "I don't like this one bit. They're up to something, and I fear it's us." He opened one of his saddlebags and retrieved two revolvers that Luka had never before laid eyes upon. Ike handed one of the guns to his brother. "Stick it under your shirt and have it ready under your blanket tonight. I fear they're waiting for us to take off our holsters when we go to bed."

"I feel the same way. I hope we're wrong."

"Better wrong than dead. Let's get the skillets and everything out before they get back."

After the men brought enough wood back to camp to start a fire, Ike began frying salted pork in the skillet and warming beans in a pot while Luka boiled coffee. Ike felt so stiff and sore that he could barely squat over the fire to cook. He dreaded going to bed and having to stay awake while he kept tabs on the men. If he could have his way, he would go to bed without supper and sleep for a day.

Leo wasn't much of a talker, but Seth was one of those men that could yap for hours without ever saying or revealing much of anything. He did have a way of sprinkling seemingly innocent questions into his ramblings. By now, Ike and Luka were convinced that Seth was working them for information in order to attempt to empty their accounts after they were dead.

If not for the fact that Ike feared he'd give away that he and Luka were aware of the men's motives, he would have told Seth to shut the hell up. He felt overjoyed when dusk finally settled over the land. He stood and threw wood into the fire, hoping to have some light for as long as possible. "Boys, it's been a long day. I need my rest," he said before spreading his bedroll. He removed his holster and hung it on the saddle horn.

The rest of the men followed suit, laying out their bedrolls and climbing into them.

After Ike crawled under his cover, he retrieved his revolver from his pants and rested it on his stomach. He closed his eyes and struggled to stay awake. He hadn't been this weary since his days of fighting the war. Luka began to snore. The noise caused Ike to curse under his breath. He could only hope that his brother was faking the sounds. In anticipation of bringing an end to their predicament, he did the same.

An hour passed before Ike heard a noise. Through the slits of his eyes, he could see Seth and Leo as they stealthily crawled out of their bedrolls. The men retrieved their revolvers and turned toward the Gunther brothers. When Ike heard the click of a hammer being pulled back, he raised his revolver and shot through his cover. In the still of the night, the roar of the gun seemed as loud as a cannon. His shot hit Seth in the belly and caused the young man to grab at his wound. The unexpected attack caused Leo to freeze in disbelief and stare at Seth while Ike continued firing his Colt.

Luka had heard the men climb out of their beds, too. As soon as Ike fired, Luka threw back his cover and took aim at Leo. Like his brother, he preferred to err on the side of caution and emptied his gun upon the men.

Seth and Leo performed a macabre dance and screamed in agony as the bullets tore into their flesh. They fell dead from multiple gunshot wounds without ever having fired their guns.

"I wondered if you were going to sleep through the whole gunfight," Ike growled as he climbed out of his bed.

"I waited for you to shoot first. I knew if I took the first shot that you would accuse me of rushing things. They're dead and we're not, so shut up," Luka fired back.

"I shot the hell out of a good blanket."

"Better you having done it than them."

"You do have a point there," Ike said. He checked the men for pulses. "They're both dead."

"I would hope so. There's nothing like a life or death situation to realize I can still hit what I aim at."

"I was ready to shoot Seth just to shut him up anyways. Those boys weren't smart enough to try to pull this off. A child could have seen through them."

"I hear that. All the same, I wish it wouldn't have come to this," Luka said.

"Me either. I'm going to say this and say it only once, and you'd better keep your mouth shut. I wasn't ready for this ride. I'm going to bed now and don't get me up in the morning. I don't care if I sleep until ten. I'll never be able to ride tomorrow otherwise."

"Can you really go to sleep after this?"

"Luka, I'm about ready to collapse," Ike said as he climbed back into his bedroll.

"This is a fine start to our journey. If we'd been a half hour earlier or later, we probably wouldn't have ever crossed paths with these two."

"Better that it happened to us than some family in a wagon. Those two were up to no good," Ike mumbled. He was snoring a moment later.

Luka threw blankets over the bodies before pouring a cup of lukewarm coffee and taking a seat by the remnants of the fire. He couldn't imagine how Ike could be so exhausted as to go right to sleep after killing a man. Sleep for himself would be a good while in coming. Even though he wasn't much of a drinker, he wished he had some whiskey to take the edge off his emotions. He hadn't killed a man since the war, and now all those old feelings about taking another man's life came rushing back. This time there really hadn't been much choice in the matter, but that didn't reassure him much. Death scared the hell out of him and he despised killing. Yet, he knew as sure as he was sitting there, he would kill Rusty and Mackey McClure when the time came.

Chapter 13

Rock Springs, Wyoming Territory

In the late afternoon, with the sun beating down on the backs of Rusty and Mackey, they rode into the town of Rock Springs in the Wyoming Territory. Since their hasty departure of Pocatello Junction, they'd spent the week winding through a mountain path that had taken them up one ridge and down the next. Sometimes the trail corkscrewed until they felt as if they were going to meet themselves. Once the brothers had traversed the worst of the mountains, they had ridden into foothills that were so bleak and lacking of vegetation that it felt as if they'd descended into hell. Their horses were worn down from the strenuous travel and thin from lack of grass.

The sight of the town caused Rusty to grin and rub his lips in anticipation of wetting his whistle with a foamy beer even though his belly growled for attention. On the previous day, their supplies had run out and they hadn't eaten since then.

"I thought we were never going to set our eyes on another living person ever again," Mackey said with relief dripping from his voice.

"I could live without another person, but I sure could use some grub and beer," Rusty replied.

"And a bath. Ma wouldn't be pleased with our appearances right now. We look and smell like dogs caught out in a thunderstorm."

"It's hard to stay pretty on the trail. We'll get cleaned up here."

Some miners walking down the street looked as black as night in a covering of coal dust. The whites of their eyes shone like beams of light on their ebony faces. A day of hard work had the men's shoulders slouching and their pace a shuffle slow.

"That has to be worse than mining gold ever thought about being," Mackey marveled.

"I don't want to do either of them. I'll stick to robbery," Rusty replied with a chuckle.

The brothers dropped the horses off at the livery stable and headed for a restaurant. They ordered T-bone steaks, stewed potatoes, and green beans. When they finished the meal, they topped it off with apple pie. The waitress brought slices that looked so big that they must have been cut into quarter of the pie servings.

"This pie reminds me of Ma," Mackey said after a couple of bites.

"Yeah, she knows how to bake – that's for sure," Rusty replied with his mouth full of dessert.

"We need to get home and buy her some nice things with the money."

"Keep down your voice. We will in due time. I wouldn't mind adding to our wealth before we head back." Broaching the subject of their money caused Rusty to reach over and touch the saddlebag holding their loot on the chair beside him.

"We don't need to get greedy."

"We have us a good stake, but it's not like we have enough to grow old on. Nobody has a clue as to who we are. We need to do the getting while the getting is good."

"Luka knows who we are. I still think you're selling him short. He might come looking for us back home."

"We've been over this before. I know we messed up, but Luka just doesn't scare me. Nevada City is our town. We'll be safe there. Marshal Kelly will see to that. He hates those damn Germans as much as I do. And besides, I keep telling you that Luka doesn't have the grit to come after us."

"I hope you're right."

"Hell, Luka won't come back home because of Alannah," Rusty said and laughed. "You know that woman ran all over him. He's as scared of her as he is of us."

Mackey chuckled. "You do have a point there. I heard he can't keep his britches up anymore after she got done chewing out his ass."

The brothers broke into a fit of giggles and had to set their forks down to keep from dropping bites of pie. Once they regained their composures and finished their dessert, they paid for their meals and went walking down the main street in search of a saloon. The two men came upon the Coal Dust Saloon. With grins on their faces, they strolled inside the establishment.

Once they were through the doors, the saloon looked nothing like they expected. If miners were allowed inside, they must have been told to go home and scrub before crossing the entrance. The place was well lit and the floor freshly scrubbed. A lone drinker clad in buckskin from head to toe stood at one end of the bar while all of the rest of the patrons seemed to be giving that person a wide berth as they gathered on the other end. Rusty and Mackey didn't care whom they stood beside as long as they got their beers. They sidled up next to the buckskin-outfitted patron and placed their orders to the smiling bartender.

"You boys must be new in town," the buckskinned drinker barked. The voice was loud and booming. It didn't sound quite feminine or masculine.

The McClures turned their heads to look at the speaker. Both of the men failed to hide their astonishment that the person beside them was indeed a woman. She was quite attractive and obviously drunk as all get out. Her mouth hung slightly open and her eyes had the vacant gaze of someone that could barely focus well enough to make eye contact.

"We just got into town," Rusty said.

"I knew I'd never seen you before. I never forget a face."

"Pleased to make your acquaintance," Mackey said.

"My name's Martha Jane Canary, but people call me Calamity Jane," she said and laughed.

Rusty pulled his head back in surprise and his mouth dropped open. Mackey grinned and slapped the bar. They'd both heard tales of the woman that could supposedly shoot, scout, and cuss as well as any man alive.

"Bartender, give this woman a drink. I've never met me a legend before now," Rusty said.

Calamity Jane grinned. She liked the attention the newcomers showered upon her. Most men tended to shun Calamity once they'd spent some time with her. When drunk, which was often, she tended to be loud and obnoxious. The running joke was that Jane had a heart of gold and the mouth of the devil. "You fellows are all right," she said. She raised her mug to the brothers and then slurped a big drink of beer.

"Let's hear of one of your adventures," Rusty said.

"Shoot, boys, my life is all an adventure. I've seen it all and done most of it. Last year, I joined a wagon train with Wild Bill Hickok and Charlie Utter to head to Deadwood. The Injuns and outlaws were as thick as mosquitoes on a hot summer night. The three of us got enough target practice in shooting those varmints that they all eventually left us alone. It got to the point where we'd see them off in the distance, out of gun range, just watching us pass by. The Injuns would hold their spears up in the air as a salute to us. That's how much they'd come to respect us. The outlaws would just stare us down, but they made sure to stay out of range of our Winchesters. I'm a right fine shot, but you ain't seen nothing until you see Wild Bill shoot his pistols. He could shoot the earlobes off a man and never graze his cheeks – that's how accurate he is."

' "That's quite a story," Mackey said, astonishment in his voice.

"That's all it is – a big ole story," one of the men called out from the other end of the bar.

The rude comment got the better of Rusty's Irish temper. He whirled toward the men, and grabbed the butt of his revolver. With his eyes squinted in a vicious stare, he paused before speaking. "I don't recall any of us speaking to you all, but the next one that opens his mouth will be answering to me. Do I make myself clear?"

The ferocious threat served its purpose. The men at the other end of the bar looked away and resumed talking amongst themselves.

Calamity was flattered by the chivalry. "Why, thank you. That was a kind thing to do," she said.

"My pleasure. So what brings you to Rock Springs?" Rusty asked.

"I used to live here and got word that an old friend was ailing. I came back to take care of her, but she died anyway. I'll soon be heading back to Deadwood." Calamity Jane looked away and made a quick swipe of her eyes with her arm.

"Sorry for your loss," Mackey said.

"I guess we've all got to die sometime," Calamity said with a forced smile. She took another sip of her beer to end the subject.

Mackey took a big guzzle from his mug. "This beer tastes mighty good. We've been on the trail long enough to grow attached to the saddle. It sure feels good to be standing, and not on the back of a horse for a change."

"What have you boys been up to?"

"We're just drifting right now. Seeing the world, I guess you could say," Rusty said.

"Have you got a place to stay?" Jane asked.

"No, not yet. We were so parched that we headed here before going to the hotel," Mackey replied.

"Come stay at my place with me. I could use some company."

"Are you sure?" Mackey asked.

"Hell yes, I'm sure. Calamity Jane may be a lot of things, but inhospitable, she is not."

"It's settled then."

The three of them continued drinking throughout the evening. Calamity Jane regaled the brothers with stories of her adventures in the wilderness. Many of the tales sounded unbelievable, but Rusty and Mackey never questioned her. They were content to be entertained and have a conversation with someone other than their sibling.

By the time they left the saloon, all of them were so drunk that they wobbled out the door. Calamity Jane led the way to a hillside in town, and walked into a dugout burrowed into its side where she lit a lamp.

"This is where I lived back in the day. Brings back a lot of good old memories so I decided to stay here again," she said.

Rusty gave Mackey a dirty look. He'd assumed they were staying in a house for the night, and he blamed his brother for accepting the offer without more information, but he wasn't about to offend Jane. "This will do just fine," he said.

Calamity made pallets for her guests, and the brothers wasted no time in dropping down upon them. Both of them were weary from all the travel, and relaxed from so much beer. They were both asleep in short order.

Mackey awakened with a start when he felt something next to him. In the pitch-black dugout, he couldn't see a thing, and his alcohol-soaked mind struggled to remember where he was or what had happened.

"Would you hold me?" Calamity Jane whispered into his ear. "A girl gets lonely on her own sometimes."

Mackey threw his arm and leg over Calamity. "Sure, Jane," he whispered.

Chapter 14

Nevada City, Colorado

Two weeks had passed since Alannah had moved into her rental home. The tension in O'Sullivan's General Store had calmed down considerably though the atmosphere remained far from normal. Nora, for her part, came to accept that Alannah had moved out of the house. She had slowly slipped into treating her daughter more or less as she always had. Connor, on the other hand, refused to come to terms with Alannah's newfound independence. He would only speak to his daughter when absolutely necessary, and then in the most perfunctory of tones.

Alannah was ecstatic over her new living arrangement, and her father's aloof behavior toward her did not faze her in the least. She went about her business in the store as she always had and refused to fall prey to his guilt-inducing behavior. When he never mentioned firing her again, she knew she'd won the battle.

The first week in the new home had been spent cleaning the place from top to bottom. The rooms now smelled fresh and clean and no longer carried the odors of the old and infirm. She had also bought paint for the walls, but hadn't worked up the nerve to tackle the project quite yet. When she got paid, she splurged and bought some brightly colored material for curtains. Her mother had surprised her and made her first visit to help sew the drapes. They had hung them together, and Alannah had acted as happy as a little girl receiving a new doll when she saw the results. The front room now had some life to it and felt more like something she could call her own.

Sometimes the quiet of living alone bothered her some and she missed making dinner with her mother, but she now could fix whatever she desired to eat. She had even begun fixing some of the German recipes that Luka's mother had taught her years ago. The dishes with their use of sausages, noodles, and vinegar had always seemed exotic to her taste buds compared to the food she'd grown up eating.

Wanda and Betty Anne paid her a discreet visit on an evening they both had off from work. They brought a pail of beer with them, and the girls stayed up late into the night, giggling and gossiping about most everyone in Nevada City. Alannah hadn't had so much fun or laughed so hard in years. After they left, she sat at her kitchen table as she adjusted to the sudden solitude. At that point, it dawned on her how little of a social life she had had since her breakup with Luka. She'd gotten way too comfortable living with her parents. She stood up to go to bed with the conviction that those days were in the past and better times lay ahead.

A loud rap on the door startled Alannah so badly that she jumped. After recovering from the surprise, her first thought was that Wanda or Betty Anne had forgotten something. She flung the door open to find Sean Murphy swaying on her doorstep.

Sean had been in her class in school and had always managed to find a way to be an annoyance to her. After he quit his education, he had followed his daddy into the mines. On most nights, he could be found in one of the local saloons getting drunk and being a nuisance.

His breath reeked of whiskey, and Alannah had to turn her head and scrunch her nose from the pungent smell.

"Sean, what are you doing here?" Alannah asked.

"Everybody is talking about you moving here all by yourself. I figured you might be lonely and need a little company," Sean said in slurred speech.

"What I need is to get to bed. You go on and get out of here and don't you come back. You're not welcome here."

"That's no way to treat an old friend." Sean barged past her and stumbled into the front room.

Alannah turned and planted her hands on her hips in a defiant pose. "You need to get out my house this instant. I'll file a complaint with Marshal Kelly if you don't leave," she threatened.

"You're wasting your breath. Grady would be on my side. It's not illegal to pay a social visit." Sean snickered as if he was playing a winning hand of cards.

"It is if I tell you to leave."

"Alannah, your problem is that you've been too long without a man. You need a little loving to keep you from turning as frosty as all the other old maids around here."

The comment incensed Alannah and she moved away from the drunk. "Sean Murphy, don't you dare touch me. I whipped you as a boy and I'll whip you again if necessary."

"I'm a sight bigger now than those days. I got the arms and shoulders of a miner. You, on the other hand, are still as skinny as ever and not much taller. You sure grew into a pretty thing though."

Sean wobbled toward Alannah and threw his arms around her. As he leaned in to kiss her, she shoved him with all her might. He stumbled backwards a couple of steps, allowing Alannah to run to the fireplace and retrieve the poker.

"Don't you come near me again," she yelled.

Sean grinned and came barreling toward her as fast as his wobbly legs would allow with his arms out to grab the poker. To his surprise, Alannah swung the rod low and caught him on the shin. He let out a bellow so loud that it hurt her ears, and he started hobbling around the room on one leg. In his drunken state, he lost his balance and crashed to the floor.

"Get out of here or I swear to God that I'll kill you," Alannah screamed.

He glared at her with eyes so ferocious that Alannah would have been scared to death if she wasn't so mad.

"I'm going to make you sorry you did that," he warned.

As Sean crawled to the sofa and began pulling himself up, Alannah charged. She swung the poker with all her strength into his back. Sean let out another ear-piercing yell.

"You bitch," Sean hollered before getting to his feet and making a retreat for the door.

The name-calling so incensed Alannah that she gave chase like a bear on the attack. Vengeance was the only thing on her mind. Sean was a step away from escape when she took a swing at his head. The blow caught him on the right temple and he dropped as if dead. Alannah stood over him, ready to give him another blow if he so much as moved. When he didn't, she panicked that she really had killed him. She jumped up and down and fanned herself. When she finally worked up the nerve, she bent down and examined Sean. His breathing sounded fine and there wasn't any blood, though his head was sporting a pretty good knot. She sighed loudly in relief that he wasn't dead, and then her anger returned over the notion that some drunk could show up at her door expecting to have his way with her.

"I bet you'll think twice before you ever mess with me again," she boasted.

Alannah marched into the kitchen and found the twine she'd used to bundle together packages when she had moved into her new home. She returned to the front room and set the spool down before grabbing Sean by the legs. With a groan, she started dragging him outside. As she strained to get him out of the house, she farted loudly. The gas expulsion caused her to giggle hysterically at the absurdity of the evening. A thirty-year-old woman that had finally moved out of her parents' home was now spending her evening drinking beer with saloon girls and fending off drunks with a poker. She managed to get Sean out into the yard and went to retrieve her twine. After she hogtied his hands and feet together, she went in search of a handkerchief and a rag. She returned and grasped his nose and chin to pry his mouth open. The effort caused her to wrinkle her face in disgust as the smell of whiskey hit her as if a bottle of the alcohol had been uncorked. She shoved the handkerchief into his mouth and then used the rag to gag him.

"We're going to be infamous in the morning," she said as she wiped her hands on her skirt.

After sauntering back into the house, Alannah changed into her nightgown. She hesitated in going to bed for fear she wouldn't be able to sleep, but reluctantly crawled under the covers. With all the excitement over with for the night, her stamina began to drain as quickly as a bucket of water with a hole in it. A few minutes later, she fell sound asleep.

In the morning, Alannah's eyes popped wide open as the previous evening's events came rushing back. She jumped out of bed and peeked out the window. Sean remained out in the yard, bound up tighter than a woman in a corset. The sight of him craning his neck around like a turtle popping its head out of its shell caused her to smile and feel relieved. She knew her conscience would have consumed her if she had killed him.

Alannah went to fix her breakfast and get ready for work. When she was ready to leave the house, she stepped outside to find Marshal Kelly and his deputy standing in the yard with the recently freed Sean.

"What's the matter, Sean? You look as ill as a man that's been hogtied and gagged by a woman," Alannah called out.

Sean took a step toward her before the marshal grabbed his arm.

Marshal Kelly turned his attention toward Alannah. "I'm going to have to arrest you for assault. From the looks of the knot on his head, you're lucky you didn't kill poor Sean," he said.

Alannah's Irish temper got the best of her and she flew into a rage. She spread her feet in a defiant pose and dug her fists into her hips. "Don't you think you should hear my side of the story before you decide who's in the wrong?" she yelled.

"Well, Sean is the one with the lump on his head."

"If you arrest me, I'll hire Saul Goldstein as my lawyer and sue you and this county for all you're worth. We'll win, too, when the truth comes out over what really happened. You won't be able to get a job as the town drunk after the county goes broke paying me off," she threatened.

The outburst got the marshal's attention, and he seemed to wither a little from the tongue-lashing. "Well, I guess I should get your side of the story," he said, and started rubbing the back of his neck and looking down at his feet.

With her hands flying for effect, Alannah launched into telling of her encounter with Sean the previous evening. When she finished, she said, "So what are you going to do now that you know the real story? You know one of us always tells the truth, and one of us is a born liar."

"Did you really find it necessary to hogtie and gag him?" the marshal asked.

"Well, I guess if I wanted to feel completely safe, I could have killed him. That would have been a permanent solution to the problem," Alannah fumed.

"Sean, is she telling the truth?" Marshal Kelly asked.

"It don't give her no right to take a fire poker to me," Sean protested.

"Sorry for the misunderstanding, Miss O'Sullivan," the marshal said meekly. He tipped his hat and grabbed Sean by the arm to escort him away.

The turn of events did little to pacify Alannah. She stormed over to the store and went inside, slamming the door as she did so. As her parents looked at her in surprise, she began recounting the previous evening's events for a second time. About halfway through her rant, she started to have second thoughts about sharing the ordeal. Her mother had turned white and was covering her mouth with her hands in horror. Worse yet, her father was beet red and looked ready to explode. Alannah had no idea if he was furious with her or Sean. She finished her story and stood there waiting for someone to speak.

"You poor thing. That's terrible," Nora said. She walked over and hugged her daughter. "Thank goodness you learned how to defend yourself against your brothers or God knows what would have happened. I shudder to even think about such things."

Connor began pounding his fist on the counter. "This is all your fault. If you would have stayed home where you belong, then none of this would have happened. A single woman on her own might as well hang a sign on her door welcoming all the scoundrels on earth into her home. We are going to be the laughingstock of all of Nevada City," he hollered.

Alannah stood looking at her father, too stunned to speak. Never in her wildest dreams would she have expected him to practically defend Sean's actions. She knew he wouldn't take the news well, but this was something entirely different. The first tears welled up in her eyes, and she felt so angry that she didn't trust what would come out of her mouth. She spun around and ran out the door. Once outside, she dropped down onto the edge of the boardwalk and began bawling.

Nora looked at her husband and shook her head in dismay. "I've known you to fly off the handle and say some addlebrained things in your time, but what you just said to your daughter takes the cake. Instead of blaming the man that came to her house looking for trouble, you managed to blame her for being in her own home and bothering no one. And then instead of being upset that she was nearly raped, you were more worried about what all the gossips in this town would say and think. I would hope our daughter's well-being would take precedence over gossip. Connor O'Sullivan, I'm ashamed of you. Your words were so out of line. You had better decide what is important to you because if you make the wrong choice, you're going to fool around and lose your daughter. That would be a terrible thing to lose because of your vanity." Before her husband could respond, Nora stormed off to the back of the store.

As Connor's fury faded, his wife's scolding began to take hold and his conscience got the better of him. He knew he'd handled the situation about as poorly as a man possibly could. As he stared at the door, he realized he needed to go find his daughter. He walked outside and was surprised to find Alannah sitting on the walk. With a sigh that sounded as if it held the burden of every regret in his life, Connor sat down beside his daughter and placed his hand on her knee.

"Alannah, I'm truly sorry. I handled that about as poorly as a father possibly could have. My first reaction should have been gratitude that you weren't harmed, and my second should have been pride that a daughter of mine could subdue a man," Connor said.

Alannah sniffled a couple of times and used her sleeve to wipe her eyes. She glanced at her father and could see all the guilt weighing on him. His eyes looked sorrowful and seemed to her to be pleading for forgiveness. "Thanks, Daddy. Apology accepted," she said.

Connor gave a paternal smile. "I made your moving out about me. After thirty years of having you in the house, I guess I was too set in my ways to let you go. With a daughter still at home, I could feel as if I wasn't so old. To be honest, this knowing that there are more days behind me than in front of me is not an easy thing to come to terms with. I won't say another word about your moving out. I hope it brings you what you are looking for."

Alannah leaned her head against her father's shoulder. "You are a long ways from being old. You and Momma have a lot of years left. And it wasn't as if I was unhappy living at home, but I just felt as if I was stuck somewhere between a child and a grown woman. I guess I just wanted some space to figure out who I am these days."

"Maybe you'll find you a good man yet. It's not too late. Marriage is a wonderful thing when it is with the right person."

Biting her lip, Alannah hesitated in responding. She didn't want to ruin the moment. Her father had given in more than she would have thought possible, and she knew that it couldn't have been easy for him to admit his faults, but he would never understand that Luka had been the right man for her. A lifetime of Catholic indoctrination would never let him understand her love for a Protestant. She guessed that maybe she was a lot like her father and set in her ways. There certainly was no reason that she couldn't fall in love again, but she also knew that the heart wants what the heart wants. Hers couldn't get past Luka. "Maybe I will find someone," she replied instead.

Chapter 15

Wyoming Territory

The McClure brothers spent two days in drunken debauchery with Calamity Jane before Rusty had his fill of the shenanigans. Mackey and Jane were getting a little too cozy for his taste, and he feared his brother might balk at leaving if things continued on the course they'd taken. Rusty also worried about what Mackey might say when soused. His brother could on occasion get weepy when drunk and would then tearfully confess to his past sins amidst worry he was going to Hell. While Rusty had no doubt that Jane was fond of the brothers, he also didn't doubt for a second that she would shoot them dead if she knew what they'd done back in Bozeman. Calamity Jane might have been a drunk, but she had her scruples.

In the morning, while Jane still slept, Rusty pushed Mackey out of the dugout and led him to a spot out of hearing range of anyone.

"What's got in your craw?" Mackey asked. He squinted and held his hand over his eyes to shield them from the bright morning light.

"As soon as Jane wakes up, we're telling her goodbye and hitting the trail. It's time to get to moving," Rusty replied.

"Ah, I ain't ready to leave. I think I'm in love with Jane."

Rusty managed to stymie a laugh. His brother's whiny voice reminded him of a horny teenager. "I don't care if you're in love with the Queen of England, we're leaving. We've already stayed longer than we should have. For all we know, we have a posse on our trail."

"I seriously doubt that. They'd already be here by now if they were still after us."

"Doesn't matter. I'm not starting a new life in this Podunk town so that you and Jane can drink yourselves to death. I'm going to go get the horses out of the livery stable. They should be well rested by now. Then I'm going to get us some supplies. We're done with this discussion," Rusty said. He turned to leave.

"But you've been just as drunk as we have," Mackey protested.

"Yes, I have, but enough is enough. What would Ma say if she knew we've been sitting around drunk as a skunk?"

"I doubt it would bother her half as much as if she knew what else we've been up to. Before we go, I want to tell Jane our real names. Maybe she'll find me some day."

"Hell no. If the law gets ahold of our real names after what we did to that freighter, we'll never be able to go home again and see Ma. Think about that."

"Who died and made you boss?"

Rusty swatted his hand through the air and stomped off toward the livery stable. By the time he returned to the dugout, Calamity Jane stood outside the dwelling with Mackey. She looked as if she was on the verge of tears. Mackey didn't look much better.

Rusty stuck out his hand to shake with Jane. "Mighty glad to get to know a legend. I'll always remember our time together," he said.

Jane grabbed Rusty's hand and shook it as vigorously as any man ever would have. "Hate to see you boys go.

We've had us some fun times these last few days." She squeezed her lips tightly together and looked away.

An awkward silence fell over the group until Mackey threw his arms out as if he was trying to catch a boulder and embraced Calamity. He leaned over and kissed her on the lips. "You take care. Maybe we'll meet up again someday," he said.

"I'll be back in Deadwood if you ever want to find me, but if you wait too long, I'm liable to finagle Wild Bill into marrying me first," Jane said. She managed a laugh.

The brothers mounted their horses and rode out of town without looking back. An hour passed without a word being spoken between them.

Mackey finally broke the silence. "Do you ever think about settling down and getting married?" he asked.

"Nah, that stuff ain't for me. We're outlaws. I've never had a hankering to do honest work. I like the life we live just fine."

"I don't know. I get tired of always being on the move. I could have been famous as Calamity Jane's husband. She's a swell woman even if she drinks too much."

"She's going to end up being the town drunk somewhere if she's not careful. And that swell woman would shoot you dead if she knew what we did to Irene Gunther – husband or not."

"I fear we'll come to regret that day. We let vengeance get the better of us. The Gunther brothers were just doing their job when they arrested us. We were stupid to ever have robbed a place that knew us in the first place."

"I don't want to hear it. Those Gunthers had it in for us since the day we met them in school. You know Germans think they're superior to the Irish."

"Let's just ride and not talk. Sometimes your hatred of Germans is just too much for me. You know as well as I do that we never tried to be friends with them."

Rusty spurred his horse into a lope in order to avoid a reply.

For the next seven days, the brothers followed the Union Pacific Railroad line to the east. As dusk settled over the landscape, they made camp a couple of miles outside of Laramie. All of the traveling had made them weary and short-tempered with each other. Both men went about gathering firewood as if they were sleepwalking.

"I don't know why we couldn't have just ridden into Laramie and got a room at a hotel and bought a hot meal," Mackey complained.

"Because we might do a little business tomorrow and I don't want the whole town seeing our faces," Rusty replied.

"I still think we need to lay low for a while."

"We'll be fine. Let me do the thinking."

"Of course, everybody always said you were the brains of the family," Mackey said sarcastically.

"No, just the one with some ambition."

"One of these days somebody is going to get suspicious with us always traveling with extra horses."

"We could be taking them to sell at the livery stable for all they know. Let's just get the food to cooking. I'm not in the mood to discuss all this."

"You'll not be happy until you get me killed," Mackey said. He stomped off into the brush in search of more firewood.

Rusty got the fire started, and dumped a can of beans into a pot that he set over the flame. As the beans began to warm, he tossed a couple of pieces of salt pork into a skillet. The sizzle of the meat frying made Rusty smile. There was something about the sound that he had always enjoyed.

Just as the meal finished cooking, Mackey returned to camp with an armload of wood. He poured cups of coffee while Rusty filled their plates with food.

Mackey took a bite of pork and chewed it thoroughly before asking, "So what kind of a place are you planning to rob tomorrow?"

"I'm thinking we need to move up to a bank like the James boys," Rusty replied with a gleam in his eyes.

"Don't you think we need more than two people to pull off a bank robbery? We won't have anyone to hold the horses."

"We'll be fine. We'll be in there and out before anybody knows what happened. Quit your worrying."

Mackey shook his head before reaching into his saddlebag and retrieving a can of peaches. "I hope you know what you're doing."

After the meal, the brothers cleaned the cooking utensils and went straight to bed. Since their camp sat so close to town, they waited the next morning until the sun had cleared the horizon before they crawled out of their bedrolls.

"I wish we could go to town for breakfast. I have a hankering for a plateful of eggs and bacon," Mackey mused.

"If today goes well, I promise you that we'll find us a mining town with plenty of gambling, girls, and whiskey to hole up in for a while. We'll have us some fun," Rusty said. To show his sincerity, he grinned and nodded his head.

"You're not ready to go home yet, are you?"

"Not really. Ma is going to be mad as all get out at us for not coming to see her as soon as we got out of prison, and she'll find a million things for us to fix so that we can't leave again."

"Let's get breakfast made and get this over with."

After a meal of jerky and hardtack, washed down with strong coffee, the brothers set off for Laramie.

"Pull your hat down low," Rusty said as they reached the edge of town.

Laramie bustled with Saturday morning shoppers walking on the boardwalks and coming in and out of shops.

"Maybe we picked a bad day," Mackey said.

"Nah, if there happens to be trouble, all these folks will just add to the confusion," Rusty assured his brother.

They passed a bank on the corner of a block. Rusty gave a nod of his head toward the building. The brothers turned down a side street and then turned again onto the street behind the bank. After tying the horses to a hitching rail, they marched like soldiers toward their destination.

"Do you have your bandana ready to pull up?" Rusty asked.

"Yes, for God's sake. I'm really not an idiot," Mackey growled.

When they reached the bank door, they pulled up their bandanas and slipped inside the building. Much to their chagrin, the bank was crowded with customers lined up in front of two tellers. Rusty and Mackey drew their guns.

"This is a robbery," Rusty yelled. "All of you men drop your gun belts onto the floor – now. Everybody get over there in the corner. Put your hands up in the air. Nobody will get hurt if you do what we ask."

A couple of women shrieked and threw their hands over their mouths. The men begrudgingly dropped their gun belts, and the crowd scurried toward the corner. With the customers out of the way, Rusty and Mackey stormed toward the tellers.

"Start filling bags with money," Rusty ordered.

Mackey's gun trembled in his hand, and the armpits of his shirt were soaked with sweat. He kept glancing toward the customers, fearing that he'd get shot in the back by someone wanting to be a hero.

The outlaw's distraction allowed the teller standing across from Mackey to pull a derringer out of his drawer and fire. The pistol had been stashed away for years and the gunpowder was old. Instead of a loud roar, the gun made a popping sound. Mackey bellowed in pain as the bullet hit his chest. He fired his revolver reflexively, hitting the teller in the forehead. The man blinked his eyes a couple of times as if he was surprised to have a bullet in his head before dropping dead like a felled tree.

Women screamed and bedlam ensued.

"How bad is it?" Rusty hollered above the din.

"Let's get the hell out of here," Mackey yelled.

The brothers bolted for the door. Before they had run ten paces down the side street, some of the customers were running out of the bank and screaming of the robbery. A deputy heard all the commotion and gave pursuit. He pulled out his revolver and fired a shot while still on the run. The bullet passed between the outlaws. Rusty and Mackey spun around and began shooting at the deputy until they finally hit him. As he fell to the ground, they resumed their getaway. They made it to their horses and galloped away to the southwest, following the Laramie River.

"So how bad are you hurt?" Rusty shouted over the clomping of the horses' hoofs.

"I guess not too bad since I can still run, but it hurts like hell," Mackey shouted.

"They're going to be coming after us for sure this time. I think we might have killed that lawman."

"I know. Any idea where we're going?"

"To those mountains in the distance. I don't have a clue as to how far away they are, but that has to be our best bet."

After riding hard for over an hour, the horses were drenched in lather and snorting air. The brothers reluctantly stopped at the edge of the river to allow the animals to drink water, and to switch up their mounts.

"Let's see your wound," Rusty said.

Mackey unbuttoned his shirt and pulled it open. The bullet glistened in the pectoral muscle. "At least it didn't go through the bone," he said.

Rusty pulled his knife from the sheath. "That wound is nothing. Here, let me pop that bullet out of there. Won't be nothing to it."

"Like hell, if you think you're going to use that knife without heating it first. There's rabbit innards on that thing. What are you trying to do – kill me?"

"Maybe you're right, but it might be a spell before we get the chance to get it out of you."

"I'll take my chances. Do you think they're on our trail by now?"

"Oh, yeah. They'll be coming for sure."

"You never listen to me. I knew this was a bad idea. I could feel it in my bones. You're liable to get us hanged this time."

"I guess you were right after all, but I got us into this and I'll get us out of it. We can outrun them. Thank goodness we know good horseflesh when we steal it," Rusty said with a snort. "We best get back to riding."

Chapter 16

Montana Trail, Montana Territory

After two weeks on the trail, Ike and Luka had been assured by other travelers they met that they were less than a day's ride away from Pocatello Junction. News of the murders and robbery of the men on the freighter had been the raging topic of everyone they met in their travels. As soon as the brothers had heard of the crime, they suspected that the culprits were the McClure brothers, but decided to keep that information to themselves. Ever since the law had failed to bring the brothers to justice, Ike had become resolute that he and Luka would be the ones that would find them.

Luka worried about Ike. All the traveling had taken its toll on his brother. Ike's cheeks and eyes looked sunken in and his color was poor. Though Ike never complained, Luka could see that his brother stayed in constant agony. He'd catch Ike wincing in pain in unguarded moments. Luka had tried to get him to stop for a day to rest, but Ike would have none of it. Ike's only respite was that Luka would make sure not to wake him in the mornings so that he got a little extra rest.

About an hour after the brothers had bedded down for the night, Luka awakened to the sound of Ike moving about the campsite. This wasn't the first time Luka had heard his brother scurrying about in the night, and the one thing Luka knew for sure was that Ike should be too exhausted to be up at that time.

Luka threw open his bedroll and sat up. "What's bothering you?" he asked.

Ike looked over in surprise that Luka was awake. "Ah, nothing really," he said.

The reply so lacked conviction that Luka stood and began throwing wood onto the fire until the flame burned bright enough to put out some decent light. When he finished, he took a seat and said, "I know that talking about things isn't easy for you, but why don't you give it a try? Maybe you'll feel better afterward."

Ike took a seat across the fire from his brother and stared down at his feet. A couple of minutes of silence went by before he nervously cleared his throat to speak. "I miss Irene and the kids so much that it hurts as much as these damn bullet holes do. Even out here in the middle of nowhere, I catch myself looking off into the distance and expecting to see them coming to join us. I know that sounds silly, but it's the truth," he said.

Luka felt the need to occupy his hands. He pulled out his knife and grabbed a stick to whittle. "Doesn't sound silly to me at all," he said. "There is no way that you can adjust to them being gone this quickly. They were here one day and gone the next. None of us expects to lose loved ones in the prime of their life. And you didn't even get to tell them goodbye. Heck, I keep looking for them, too."

"Do you really?"

"I sure do."

Ike nodded his head thoughtfully. "I'm also tortured thinking about the fear that they had to feel in their final moments. A person should get to leave this earth in peace. Can you imagine the terror they felt? And the humiliation that Irene experienced?" Ike's voice broke and he jammed his fist against his lips.

Luka dropped the stick and rubbed his chin with the palm of his hand as he tried to come up with some comforting words. He quickly realized that there were none. "I know. I've thought about all that a lot, too. I don't have any answers to any of that. They died horrible deaths. That's all there is to it."

With his fist still jammed against his mouth, and his eyes scrunched together, Ike rapidly nodded his head. He loudly sucked in a breath of air in an attempt to stymie a cry. "I wasn't much of a husband or father either. I spent all my time thinking about the ranch. Sometimes, I was brusque and hateful with Irene for no reason other than I was in an ill mood. And I didn't spend near enough time with the children. Heck, you spent more time playing with them than I ever did. What does that say about me?"

"It makes you human is what it does. None of us are always our best selves with our loved ones. That's just human nature. Look at how we get on each other's nerves sometimes. And don't forget how much we struggled with getting the ranch going. That's a lot of pressure. You know that Irene and I were close. She talked to me about you sometimes, and believe me, she understood what you were going through. You were the love of her life – believe me when I say that. She never regretted a day with you. As for the kids, maybe you could have spent more time with them, but they adored you. You were far better with them than you are giving yourself credit for being. Beating yourself up won't accomplish anything. Just keep your mind on finding Rusty and Mackey. That's all we can do at this point."

Ike let out a sigh that sounded as if he'd emptied his lungs of air. "I just don't know – I don't know. I suppose you're right, but not thinking about all this is easier said than done. My family is dead and I don't know how to go on."

"The first thing you need to do is start taking care of yourself. To be honest, you don't look well. You've lost a lot of weight since we left home. I know you're in a lot of pain, too. I can see it in your face. When we get to Pocatello Junction, I think we need to take a day to rest. What do you say?"

"Maybe we will. I suddenly feel more exhausted than ever. Let's get back to bed. I think I can sleep now. And Luka – thanks for the talk. You're a good brother – most of the time," Ike said, and even managed a faint smile.

"You're not too bad yourself," Luka said before climbing back into his bedroll.

The brothers were both snoring a few minutes later.

Ike, for the first time in a week, beat Luka out of bed the next morning. He had the fire rekindled, and the coffee over the flame by the time Luka stirred from his slumber.

"You're up early. How are you feeling?" Luka asked. He climbed out of his bedroll and stretched.

"Pretty good. I slept well for a change. Our talk seemed to help at least for one night. My chest doesn't even hurt this morning. I think once I don't have to spend all day on a horse that I'll get back to being my old self," Ike replied.

Luka concealed his surprise at Ike's lengthy reply. His brother had already said more than he usually did by noon. "That's good to hear. Are you making breakfast too?" he asked with a grin.

"I am. The sooner we get to Pocatello Junction, the better. I'm going to have me a hot bath and get a shave."

"That sounds good to me."

After the brothers finished their meal, they wasted no time in breaking camp and hitting the trail. They arrived in Pocatello Junction midmorning.

"Well, damn. Nobody told us this place wasn't much more than a shantytown," Ike groused.

"I have to admit that I find the amenities a little lacking for the life I've come to expect," Luka joked.

Ike stopped his horse in front of a trading post where a man worked at sweeping the boardwalk as if his life depended on it. "Anywhere we can get a hot bath and a shave?" he asked.

The man stopped his chore and looked up at the brothers. His expression gave away that he was clearly sizing them up before answering the question. "My wife is inside. Tell her I said it was all right. We got a tent in the back for such things," he said before resuming his sweeping.

The brothers exchanged glances, and Luka arched his eyebrows in dismay. "Friendly little place they have here," he said.

"Does this place have a hotel?" Ike asked, causing the storeowner to stop his task once again.

"Just a room full of cots that you can rent."

Ike looked at Luka and shook his head. "There's no need to put our horses up in the livery stable then. I'm not staying in a room full of farting miners. I'd rather sleep on the ground. Let's get cleaned up and get out of here."

"Sounds good to me," Luka replied.

After tying their horses in front of the trading post, the brothers walked up onto the boardwalk. Luka spotted a wanted poster for the freighter robbery tacked up on the wall. The Long Haul Freighter Company was offering a two thousand dollar reward for the capture of those responsible for the murders and robbery of their freighter crew. The poster had sketches of two men on it. While the drawings weren't accurate enough that a stranger would ever be able to pick the McClure brothers out of a crowd, Luka recognized that it was them. He pointed at the poster for Ike to see.

Ike turned to the store proprietor. "On the trail, we heard that nobody had a clue as to who committed the robbery. Were they wrong?"

The man stopped his sweeping once again and let out a sigh that would have gotten him throttled if Ike hadn't wanted a bath so badly.

"Two men showed up here a few days after the robbery. A miner accused one of them of cheating at cards and drew down on him. The other fellow shot him in the back. Killed him dead. Probably would have been ruled justifiable if they hadn't shot up the town making a getaway. Now they're charged with murder except nobody has any idea who they were. Everybody just figures they were the same ones that robbed the freighter. Now can I finish my sweeping or do you want to talk all day?"

Ike ignored the curt reply. "Any idea which direction they ran?"

"They rode north out of town. Some of the men tried tracking them the next day. They followed them east for a bit and then lost them."

"Much obliged."

Inside the trading post, the brothers found the owner's wife to be much more hospitable. She led them out back and began filling tubs with water heated over a raging fire. After the brothers climbed into the tubs, the woman came back to retrieve their clothes to wash them.

Ike leaned his head back against the tub and let out a sigh. "This feels so good that I could stay in here forever."

Ignoring his brother's comment, Luka said, "That was Rusty and Mackey. We're never going to find them now that they've left the trail. Who knows where they'll show up next."

"I know it was them, and I know how we'll find those two."

"How?"

"They'll eventually go home. We need to be there when they do."

"We don't even know if Miss McClure is still alive. They won't have any reason to go back if she's dead."

"We can ride on down to Ogden to send a telegram to Nevada City to find out if she's still alive. If she is, we can take the train from Ogden to Cheyenne," Ike said.

"I don't know. That's a long ways to go on a hunch. I swore I'd never go back to that place. You know all those Irishmen hate us," Luka grumbled.

Ike let out a laugh. "I don't think it's all those Irishmen that you're worried about. I think it is one particular Black Irish lady that has you concerned."

Luka looked at his brother and gave him a scowl. "That's very funny. For your information, I hadn't even given Alannah a thought."

Grinning and shaking his head in disbelief, Ike said, "I hate to say so, but I have to believe that was a damn lie. Alannah never ever got out of your mind or you would've found somebody else by now. The pickings in Bozeman might be a little slim, but they aren't nonexistent."

Luka sputtered as he tried to defend himself. "All right, maybe she did cross my mind when you mentioned going back to Nevada City, but I got over her a long time ago. If you'd been through all I went through with that woman, you wouldn't ever want to cross paths with her again either. She should marry the Catholic Church. God knows she would never be content with a lowly Lutheran."

Ike started laughing again. "Ain't love grand?"

"That's not funny and you know it. She broke my heart. Now let's change the subject. I'll tell you one thing we need to do if we're going to chase them back into civilization – we need to pay a visit to U.S. Marshal Tompkins and have him deputize us as deputy marshals. Otherwise, we're liable to get ourselves into trouble when the bullets start flying. We need to make sure this is all nice and legal."

"That's a good idea. I keep you around for that head on your shoulders."

"Well, at least we can agree on something," Luka said. He took a deep breath and disappeared under the water.

Chapter 17

Mountains Southwest Of Laramie

Mackey was getting sicker by the day from his injury. After the bank robbery attempt, the brothers had made it into the mountain range, and despite his fever, they had continued to follow the winding passes for days, stopping only at nightfall. They only had the luxury of a campfire on one night when they made camp high in the mountains in a basin that shielded the flames from view. Rusty had scrubbed his knife and sterilized it in the fire before removing the bullet from Mackey's chest, but the wound had already festered by that time. Mackey's fever had been getting worse ever since, and he had even babbled nonsense a few of times.

On a couple of occasions when they had been atop a summit, Rusty had used his spyglass to catch sight of the posse still on their trail. The riders were gaining on them. With his brother's deteriorating condition, he feared he'd soon be faced with the decision of whether to leave Mackey behind or surrender together. His dilemma had kept him awake into the night as he struggled with whether survival trumped loyalty. Their ma would never forgive him if he left Mackey behind, but he wondered if she'd prefer one alive son or two hanged ones.

The brothers finally made it through the mountain range to the North Platte River. Traveling became much easier, but they would be caught out in the middle of nowhere if the posse found them. Mackey could barely sit upright in the saddle. He didn't complain, but Rusty doubted his brother could go much farther.

As they rounded a bend in the river, Rusty spotted a buckskin-clad man standing on the river's edge. The man busily worked a cane pole back and forth across the water in an attempt to catch trout. He had long hair and a long beard, and wore a revolver tucked in his belt and a fishing basket around his neck.

"You stay here," Rusty said as he climbed down from his mount.

Mackey nodded his head and slumped over his horse to rest.

When Rusty got within shouting distance of the mountain man, he called out, "Hey there. I mean you no harm, but I would like to have a word with you."

The man whipped his head toward the sound of the voice and dropped his pole to rest his hand on his revolver. "I have nothing to steal, if that's what you're after. You best watch yourself," he hollered.

A closer look at the man surprised Rusty. The fisherman looked to be no older than maybe forty. He was of medium height with muscles bulging under his clothes.

"I have no reason for trouble." Rusty held his arms out away from his body as he continued walking.

"What can I do for you?" the mountain man asked when Rusty neared him.

"I'm just going to be honest with you. My brother and I tried to rob a bank in Laramie. He got shot and is sporting a bad fever. The wound isn't serious except it has festered. We have a posse on our tail. I'll give you a hundred dollars in gold coins if you'll hide us and help me nurse my brother back to health."

The mountain man looked over Rusty's shoulder toward Mackey. "How do I know I can trust bank robbers?" he asked.

The question brought a smile to Rusty's face and he knowingly nodded his head. "We're desperate and you're our only hope. I'd be willing to surrender our guns if it'll make you feel better."

"How far behind is the posse?"

"I think maybe a couple of hours, but I'm not sure."

"I don't owe you a thing. I'd be taking a risk for someone that I don't know from Adam."

"No, you don't, but I'll owe you. I'm not about to cause trouble with the man that saves our necks. I may not be the most honest man you've ever met, but I'm not the kind that doesn't appreciate a favor."

While the man pondered his decision, he glanced over at Mackey one more time. "Go get your brother."

The mountain man mounted his horse and was waiting in the middle of the river by the time that Rusty and Mackey joined him. They followed him to the north for a couple of miles until they were back in the foothills. After leaving the river, they wound through the hills for another mile until they came upon a cabin with smoke drifting from the fireplace.

"My squaw is in there. You boys had better be on your best behavior. If you don't fear me, you ought to fear her. She can be a mean one," the mountain man said.

"Do you have a name?" Rusty asked.

"You can call me Dan. She goes by Dalilah."

"I'm Rusty, and he's Mackey. I'd appreciate you keeping that amongst yourselves."

Dan let out a chuckle. "I don't have many conversations with other folks these days, and I don't think I'll be giving you away after I aid you outlaws."

"Do you think they can find us here?"

"Nobody has found me yet. You might not be the only one with things to hide."

Dan led the brothers into the cabin. "Dalilah, we have company. This man needs your help," he said, gesturing toward Mackey. "He's been shot and his wound has festered."

The Indian woman looked right pretty with delicate features and high cheekbones. She looked to be about the same age as Dan. Her small frame was attired in a store-bought cotton dress that she wore with moccasins. She studied the strangers intently, and her face gave away no sign as to what she thought about the new arrivals.

"Go get on the cot," Dalilah ordered in a husky voice with near perfect sounding English.

Mackey ambled over to the bed and stretched out on it. Without saying another word, Dalilah came over and started unbuttoning his shirt. She exclaimed something in her native tongue that sounded as if she might be swearing.

"Heat your knife," she said to Dan.

Dan pulled his knife from its sheath and held it over a candle until satisfied the blade was sterilized. He gently handed it to Dalilah. She waved it through the air of few times to cool before making an X cut across the wound. The knife was so sharp and her actions so fast that she had completed her task before Mackey even had time to wince.

"Be still now while I work," Dalilah told Mackey.

Dalilah began squeezing pus from the wound. Her actions caused Mackey to grit his teeth and scrunch up his face in pain, but he held still and never made a sound. When she finished, she wiped the wound with a cloth and went off to make a poultice.

When Dalilah finished making the medicine, she returned to Mackey. "This will make the wound better," she said as she packed the wound with the yellow yarrow compress.

"Thank you," Mackey said.

"You should thank Dan. He's the one that brought you to our home. I will make willow bark tea for your fever now."

Dalilah went to the stove to begin boiling willow bark in water.

"So are you a trapper?" Rusty asked Dan.

"I'm a trapper, hunter, fisherman, and about anything else that you can think of that puts food on the table and a little money in my pocket," Dan replied.

"Must get kind of lonely out here with just Dalilah."

"We keep each other company, and I'm a loner by nature. This place suits us just fine," Dan said before deciding to change the subject. "So I take it that you and your brother aren't much good at robbing banks."

Rusty couldn't help but grin even if he had been insulted. "A bank teller tried to be a hero and shot Mackey. Good thing the gun misfired or my brother would likely be dead. I might have to do a little more planning on my next one. That bank teller won't be playing hero anymore though."

"Outlaws always end up dead when it's all said and done."

"Don't we all," Rusty said and laughed.

After Dalilah had boiled the bark, she strained it into a cup and brought it to Mackey after it cooled. "Drink all of this," she ordered.

Mackey looked into the cup. "Looks like blood," he said skeptically.

"Drink it."

With a tip of the cup, Mackey gulped down the tea in one long drink. He made a face when he finished. "Doesn't taste any better than it looks," he said.

"You will have to drink more of it, so get used to it," Dalilah responded.

"Good to know."

Dalilah turned to Rusty. "He will be much better in the morning."

"Thank you for your kindness. We certainly owe you," Rusty replied.

Dan put his arm around Dalilah's shoulders. "Rusty and Mackey are paying us right smartly for your troubles. We'll have to use our best china," he joked.

"I guess that includes feeding them then," Dalilah said. She scurried away to grab Dan's fishing basket and headed outside to clean the fish.

Mackey got up to join the others for a meal of trout, bread, and some kind of green that looked like boiled spinach but tasted nothing like it. Afterward, he went straight back to the cot and slept. The only time he awoke was when Dalilah roused him to insist he drink some more willow bark tea.

Rusty kept nervously walking over and looking out the window.

"You should quit your worrying," Dan said. "If they were out there, you're going to get yourself shot, but the only way they could find us is if they have an Indian scout, and I doubt they took the time to round up one when they set upon your trail."

"I suppose," Rusty said and sat down. "So what did you do that put you out here in the mountains?"

"I killed a man in a bar fight. That was years ago and in a far different place. I don't need to hide any longer. I just prefer this life now."

Rusty grinned. "I guess I prefer the saloons and the women in them too much for this kind of life."

Dan shrugged. "I need to feed the chickens before dark." He lifted himself out of his chair and walked out of the cabin.

Dalilah remained sitting in a chair and staring at Rusty. Her gaze began making him uncomfortable. The thought crossed his mind that she might be putting a spell on him. He'd heard that some Indians had magical powers that they could cast upon a man.

"What is it?" Rusty finally asked.

"Your brother would have gotten blood poisoning if he'd gone another day without medicine. He likely would have died," Dalilah replied.

"Well, there wasn't anything I could do about that out in the middle of the mountains. He should have kept his eyes on the bank teller so that this never happened in the first place. I don't need you blaming me."

Dalilah rolled her eyes. "You don't want to mess with me."

The threat caused Rusty to lean back in his chair and eye the Indian woman warily. "I didn't mean nothing by that. I guess I'm feeling guilty for him getting shot. The robbery was my idea and he didn't want no part of it."

"You should go to a place you have never been before and start a new life. Otherwise, I see a tragic end to the lives of you and your brother."

Rusty had never been fond of Indians in the first place, and this one gave him goosebumps and chills. He thought about bolting for the door and decided better of it. Showing weakness was the last thing he wanted to do in front of the woman. "Thank you for the advice and for treating my brother," he said instead.

Dalilah nodded her head and didn't speak again.

Soon after nightfall, everyone went to bed after Dalilah plied Mackey with tea one final time for the evening. Rusty had to sleep on the floor, but he didn't mind. At least inside the cabin he didn't have to worry about bugs or snakes.

In the morning, Dalilah checked on her patient before she began cooking breakfast. She bent over the still sleeping Mackey and placed her lips on his forehead. The fever had broken, and she smiled ever so slightly.

Mackey opened his eyes. "You smell good," he said.

"Well, you don't," Dalilah shot back.

She opened Mackey's shirt and removed the yarrow poultice. The wound no longer looked an angry red, but instead had turned a healthy pink with no pus. "You are going to live, at least for a while longer," she said.

"I feel like that might be so," Mackey replied.

Dalilah turned to Rusty. "He needs to rest here for a few days to get his strength back and to make a good scab to protect the wound. After that, you can resume your foolish life."

Rusty smiled and nodded his head. "Thank you so much. Maybe we'll even take your advice. By the way, how did you get so good at talking English?"

With a wicked looking smile, Dalilah said, "White men like to hear themselves talk. If you spend enough time with them, you can learn it all."

Chapter 18

Nevada City, Colorado

The news of Alannah knocking Sean Murphy silly and hogtying him in her yard had spread like a wildfire throughout Nevada City. To Alannah's surprise, most of the gossip did not hold her responsible for causing the incident by having the audacity to live alone. She even kind of liked her newfound celebrity. Almost every woman that came into the store made a point to seek her out to commiserate on the trials of dealing with men.

Things inside the store were also much better. Connor had stuck to his word and no longer resented Alannah for having moved out of their home. With the three family members back to being their normally cheery selves, customers had noticed that the store felt homey again. Between Alannah's notoriety and the restored harmonious atmosphere, the O'Sullivan General Store had its best week of business ever.

The Colorado Mining Company had recently hired a new mining engineer from back East. The young man was still trying to get settled into his new home and made frequent trips to the general store for goods he needed. On his first visit, he had introduced himself as Mark Walsh. He was friendly and quick with a laugh. Nora was the first to notice that Mark always managed to procure Alannah's help in searching out his purchases.

When Mark walked out of the store one afternoon, Nora rushed over to her daughter. "That boy has eyes for you. He goes straight in your direction every time he comes in here."

Alannah rolled her eyes. "Oh, Momma, I think you're imagining things. He's probably just more comfortable with someone closer to his own age," she said.

"Nonsense, I see the way he lights up around you. And his name is Walsh. I bet he comes from a good Irish family, and he has a college degree to top it off. That's a mighty rare thing in this town. You should flirt with him a little bit."

"I'll do no such thing. I can't believe you expect me to act like some kind of trollop in the store. Even if he does have eyes for me, I'm not interested in someone that needs coaxing to work up his nerve to let me know how he feels. I'm interested in men, not boys."

Nora placed her hands on her hips and shook her head. "Oh, Alannah, you'll never marry a man with an attitude like that. Sometimes love needs a little push. I wasn't suggesting that you unbutton your blouse for crying out loud. You're going to get rigid in your old age if you're not careful. A man isn't a list that has to have all the boxes checked before you decide whether he's a keeper."

Alannah held her tongue, but couldn't help thinking that Luka Gunther checked a whole lot of boxes except for the one in big bold capital letters that read "Catholic". "Maybe I'm already to the point of being hopeless, but I'm really happy these days. So everything is just fine."

"Whatever, but you have to admit that Mark is one good-looking man. Nice and tall with that dark wavy hair and strong Irish chin. He's definitely a looker."

Alannah giggled. "Yes, Momma, we can at least agree on that. Mark is a handsome man."

"Finally, I've gotten you to agree to something. I'm going to quit with a victory," Nora said with a wink. She turned and stalked back to the counter before Alannah could reply.

At Mass that Sunday, Alannah had to stifle a groan when her mother enthusiastically elbowed her in the ribs when Mark Walsh walked into the church.

"I knew that boy came from a good Irish home," Nora whispered. "How many other men involved with the mines do you see in here?"

"Yes, Mother, you are always right," Alannah whispered sarcastically.

"That only took thirty years to hear."

At the first opportunity after the service ended, Nora grabbed Alannah by the hand and made a beeline to Mark.

"Mr. Walsh, so good to see you at Mass," Nora greeted. "I knew you had to be a good Catholic the first time I ever laid eyes upon you."

"Hello, Mrs. O'Sullivan. Good to see you, too. I meant to get here sooner than I have, but between moving across the country and this new job, I haven't found the time. I know that's no excuse, but it's the truth," Mark said.

"I'm just glad you came. You remember my daughter, Alannah."

"Yes, of course. I'm probably her best customer lately." Mark nodded his head at Alannah and smiled.

"Excuse me, I need a word with Mrs. Curry," Nora said before darting away, leaving Alannah and Mark to themselves.

"So how have you been, Miss O'Sullivan?" Mark asked.

"Please call me Alannah. I've been fine. I recently moved into my own place, and like you, I'm trying to get settled in."

"So I've heard. Your encounter with the drunk is all the talk at the mine. You're kind of famous in the bowels of earth. I'll be sure to run if I ever see you with a poker in your hands."

Alannah grinned in embarrassment. "So did he. It just didn't do him any good."

The couple laughed.

"Seriously, I'm glad that you are all right."

"Yes, it was kind of scary, but my Irish temper saved the day."

Mark smiled and took a big breath as if attempting to fortify himself. "I know this probably isn't the place or time to ask this, but I was wondering if I could call on you this afternoon. I thought maybe we could go for a walk or something, and then have dinner afterward."

The invitation took Alannah by surprise. She pulled her head back and hesitated in answering. No one had certainly ever asked her out at church before now. For the life of her, she didn't know what to say. "Sure. That sounds lovely," she finally replied.

"How about I come get you at around two o'clock?"

"That would be fine." Alannah gave Mark her address before parting.

Nora came rushing up to her daughter. "What were you two talking and laughing about?" she asked.

"You could have stuck around if you were so interested in the conversation." Alannah teased.

"Just tell me."

"Your little matchmaking trick worked. We're going for a walk and dinner this afternoon. Wait until you get home to begin patting yourself on the back. Pride in one's self is frowned upon in the Bible."

"You are incorrigible is what you are. You two would make beautiful babies."

"Oh my goodness. You are unbelievable is what you are. I'm going home now before you really embarrass me. You're liable to start telling me where babies come from at any moment now."

Alannah returned to her home to await Mark's arrival. She stood in front of her mirror for ten minutes as she debated whether to keep on the dress she wore to Mass or to change into something else. After changing outfits three times, she finally settled on a black skirt, white blouse, and a waistcoat. She took one more look at herself and decided that for better or worse her appearance was as good as it gets.

As much as Alannah was loath to admit it, she felt a little excited and nervous over her visit from Mark. With his fine manners and education, he certainly wasn't like most of the men in town. She worried she might not have the intellect or wit to engage with him. And this would be the first time that a man had called on her since she'd moved into her own place. The whole thing seemed a bit overwhelming.

Mark arrived promptly at two o'clock on the nose still wearing his church clothes sans the tie.

"Hello, Mark. You are a punctual man I see. What am I to make of that?" Alannah greeted.

"Probably that I am a man in need of company. Hi, Alannah," Mark said with a chuckle.

"Shall we walk?"

Mark held out his arm for Alannah to take and they started walking down the street.

"So how long have you lived here?" he asked.

"We moved here in 1859. That was the year that the town was founded. I guess I was twelve. Oh, I'm giving away my age now. They called it Nevadaville back then. Two years later the whole place nearly burned to the ground. The men got some TNT from the mine and blew up buildings to make a fire line. We were lucky in that our home and store were spared. Before we moved here, we had a store in Denver that was just getting by. Daddy saw a chance for a new life, and his decision to move here proved correct," Alannah replied.

"Sounds like quite the adventure. I promise I haven't done the math in my head to figure out your age, but whatever it is, you do look lovely."

"Why, thank you. Since we're handing out compliments, you look handsome yourself. Where are you from?"

"Boston – born and bred. I got my degree in mining engineering and worked for a couple of mines in Massachusetts. When this offer came up to come out here, it proved just too good to ignore. I was ready for something different anyway, and I've always had a fascination with the West. So here I am."

"You must think you've been stuck out in the middle of nowhere. I bet you miss the museums, the culture, and the fine restaurants. Nevada City doesn't have much of anything."

"Honestly, I may in time, but right now I have my hands full with the mine and trying to furnish a home. The mine needs modernization, and they are not being very receptive to my ideas. I'm meeting a good deal of resistance. And if I was smart, I should have moved into a boarding house, but I didn't want to share a home with a bunch of strangers. It takes some work to furnish a house from scratch."

"I was lucky that my home came furnished. I just had to get rid of that old person smell," Alannah said with a laugh.

"Well, show me around and tell me all the secrets of Nevada City."

The couple walked around the town for an hour while Alannah did most of the talking as she filled Mark in on the history and gossip of Nevada City. When they reached the City Restaurant, they went inside the establishment. Only a few customers sat at the tables at such an early dining hour, but Alannah watched as the women nodded their heads toward the couple and whispered to their companions. She figured by this time tomorrow that she would once again be the talk of the town.

Once they were seated and had time to read the menu, Alannah ordered fried chicken, mashed potatoes with gravy, and peas while Mark chose a steak, potato, and greens. Their talking hit a lull once they were amongst other people and the couple struggled to make conversation while waiting for the food to arrive. Both were relieved when the meal was served.

After a couple of bites of steak, Mark asked, "How has a pretty thing like you managed to stay single?"

Alannah looked up from her plate with her eyebrows arched in surprise at the bold question. "I don't know. I probably have a mean streak in me that runs off everybody. I've been told I'm not an easy person to be around."

"I don't believe that. You seem plenty nice to me, and I consider myself an excellent judge of character. I bet there's more to the story."

She didn't know what to say to that and thought about changing the subject before deciding just to be honest. "There was somebody at one time, but he wasn't a Catholic, and in my family, a spouse has to be a Catholic. He moved away some years ago. I guess I've never found anybody since him that could win over my heart."

"That sounds more believable. At least I can't be eliminated on my religious beliefs."

Alannah colored a little at the statement. "What about you?" she quickly asked to direct the conversation away from herself.

"I'm afraid I have let a career get in the way of my romantic pursuits. Maybe I just have never met the right girl either."

"Maybe not," Alannah said. She couldn't help but grin at him.

"Thank you for agreeing to see me today. I've had a wonderful time."

"Me too. It sure beats the painting I planned on attempting this afternoon."

The couple continued to make small talk during the meal. They discovered they both had a love for the poems of William Blake even if some of his writing seemed to clash with Catholic doctrine. When they finished eating, Mark paid the bill and opened the door for Alannah. "After you," he said.

They walked back to Alannah's house where an awkward pause ensued as the couple stood on the doorstep. Mark fumbled his words at saying goodbye before taking a loud breath. He leaned over and kissed Alannah lightly on the lips. "Thank you again for a wonderful time. May I call on you again?" he asked.

Alannah gave him a devilish grin. "I'll let you know when you ask. I had a nice time, too," she said before disappearing into the house.

Once inside, Alannah leaned her back against the door. She could feel her heart racing in her chest and she felt flush. No man since the days of Luka had made her feel the way she felt at that moment. She was giddy with excitement and stood there grinning like a fool. "Momma might have gotten something right for a change," she said aloud.

Chapter 19

Denver, Colorado

The Gunther brothers had traveled to Ogden where Ike had sent a telegram to a deputy he still trusted back in Nevada City. A couple of hours later, the brothers learned that Miss McClure was still living. Convinced that the McClure brothers would eventually return home to see their mother, Ike and Luka had their horses boarded on a livestock car, and left Ogden at midnight on a Union Pacific Railroad train. Forty hours and a couple of delays later, they arrived in Cheyenne where they boarded a Denver Pacific Railway train bound for Denver. Ike hadn't been able to confirm that their horses had been moved to the new train, and he fretted the whole trip about the animals until he arrived in Denver and retrieved their mounts and the packhorse.

"That's the way to travel," Luka said as they rode their horses toward a livery stable. "It sure saves time and my butt in the saddle."

"You won't get any argument from me. I nearly feel back to my old self after a couple of days off Nate's back."

Luka glanced over at his brother. "You're starting to look like your old self, too. You have your color back. We need to get a big steak down you now so you put some weight back onto those bones. You're too skinny."

After leaving the horses at the stable, the brothers walked to a restaurant and ordered beefsteaks.

As they were waiting for their meals, Ike said, "What are we going to do if Marshal Tompkins won't deputize us? You know he can be a cantankerous man when he wants to be."

"I don't know why you're worrying yourself so much today. First you got yourself all worked up about the horses, and now this. I don't think the marshal is going to be unsympathetic to what you've been put through. We can also mention that we believe they are involved in other crimes and murders. Marshal Tompkins isn't going to want that kind of thing happening in his territory."

"I suppose."

"If he won't do us the favor, we'll get Rusty and Mackey as bounty hunters. I have their wanted poster in my pocket."

"Where'd you get that?"

"Let's just say that Pocatello might have a wall missing a poster."

Ike managed a sad smile. "I guess I am worrying too much. Luka, I just feel lost now. Even if we get Rusty and Mackey, what do I have to live for after that? My world is gone."

"I know it is. We'll just take it a step at a time in starting over. You owe Irene and the kids that much. You can't quit living because of what has happened. They wouldn't want that for you."

The waitress returned to the table with the food, and the conversation halted as they ate their steaks.

Halfway through the meal, Ike set the forkful of meat he was about to eat back down onto the plate. "Promise me that you'll bury me with my family if I happen to die in Nevada City," he said.

The comment gave Luka a chill, and he pulled his shoulders back to keep from shuddering. "Don't say such things. We're going to get those bastards and then ride home with our heads held high. We've always been a team, and we will be after all this is done and over with."

"Promise me."

"Ike, I promise that I'll bury you right beside Irene if such a thing comes to pass."

Ike nodded his head and shoved the steak into his mouth.

After the meal, they checked into a nearby hotel. With darkness setting in, they walked to a saloon and had a couple of beers apiece before retiring for the night.

In the morning, Ike felt so nervous about meeting the marshal that he arose at first light. He badgered Luka until his brother gave up on getting any more sleep and got up to get dressed. They had breakfast finished by seven o'clock and spent an hour drinking coffee before heading to the U.S. Marshal's office.

A deputy sitting at his desk greeted the brothers when they walked into the building. "Can I help you?" he asked.

Luka figured that Ike felt too nervous to talk so he took the lead. "We were hoping we could see Marshal Tompkins," he said.

"Do you have an appointment?"

"No, but we know the marshal from way back."

"He isn't in the habit of seeing anyone without an appointment."

"Would you please just tell him that Ike and Luka Gunther are here," Luka said testily. "If he won't see us, we'll leave, but I'm not going anywhere until you check."

The deputy wrinkled his forehead and pursed his lips before reluctantly leaving his chair. He walked over to an office, opened the door, and addressed the marshal.

U.S. Marshal Charles Tompkins emerged a moment later. He was a tall, thin man dressed in a black coat and string tie. His bushy mustache had turned gray since the brothers had last seen him, and he was starting to show his age. "I thought you boys had left the fine state of Colorado for the wilds of the Montana Territory," his voice boomed out.

"We couldn't stay away from you," Luka joked.

The brothers shook the marshal's hand before he led them into his office and shut the door. The marshal's war-injured hip ached that morning, and he gingerly lowered himself into his plush leather chair. Back in the war, the Gunther brothers had served under Marshal Tompkins, and the men spent a few minutes reminiscing about the old days.

"So to what do I owe this pleasure?" the marshal finally asked.

Ike cleared his throat and began telling the marshal all that had happened to his family. As he talked, the marshal set his jaw and stroked his mustache. By the time Ike finished talking, the marshal's face was contorted in rage and as red as a beet.

"That's a damn monstrosity. Ike, you have my sincerest condolences. I really feel for you," Marshal Tompkins said. "What can I do?"

Ike faltered in speaking, so Luka spoke. "We figure they'll eventually go back to Nevada City to see their ma. We would like you to deputize us so that it's all legal."

"I see."

"We also think they have committed other robberies and murders. They're bound to hit somewhere else again."

Marshal Tompkins leaned back in his chair and resumed stroking his mustache. "If I were to do that, you boys would have to do it by the law. You can't just go in there and gun them down even if that's what they deserve. Otherwise, there'd be hell to pay for all of us."

"We understand," Ike said.

"I'll do it, but I have a favor to ask of you, too. Nevada City has gone wild ever since you boys left office. Somebody is getting shot in a saloon all the time. I want you to go in there and clean up the town."

Luka straightened his posture. "I don't imagine the sheriff of Gilpin County nor City Marshal Kelly would be too fond of that idea," he said.

"The sheriff has his hands full with Central City and the rest of the county. I'll telegraph him and let him know what's going on. He won't cross me. As for Marshal Kelly, I don't give a damn what he thinks. He's most of the problem there. If you have to, go ahead and lock him up in his own jail. That town is a blight on my territory and bad for business – my business in particular."

"We'll do it," Luka said.

Ike looked over at his brother with an annoyed expression. "I already cleaned that town up once. I wasn't planning on doing it again."

The marshal leaned forward and rested his elbows on his desk. "At the beginning of this fine day I wasn't planning on making you deputy marshals either, but here we are."

Ike smiled for the first time since they'd entered the office. "That's a good point. Let's get deputized."

The marshal deputized Ike and Luka, and they walked out of the office sporting their shiny new U.S. Deputy Marshal badges. The deputy they had first encountered did a double take when he saw the badges, but held his tongue.

Once the horses were retrieved from the livery stable, Ike and Luka headed due west toward Nevada City. They had about a two-day ride in front of them before they reached the town.

As they maneuvered through the streets of Denver, Luka said, "I've been thinking that the marshal did us a favor by asking us to clean up Nevada City."

"How so?"

"Now we don't have to tell anyone our real reason for going home. That way nobody will be trying to let Rusty and Mackey know that we're waiting for them."

"Somebody might still tell them we're there," Ike reasoned.

"Not likely. They aren't staying anywhere long enough to get a letter, and I doubt their ma would mention it in a telegram."

"That's all good points."

"Of course it is. Momma always said I was the one that got the brains."

"I never once heard Momma say such a thing."

"She also said you were the sensitive one and couldn't bear to know such things," Luka joked.

Ike shook his head and sighed when he realized his brother was pulling his leg. "Well, I know which one of us is the wiseacre," he said.

After the brothers were out of Denver, Ike began to relax. Getting deputized by the marshal had made it seem as if Rusty and Mackey's days on the loose would be over with soon. Not only was he the healthiest he'd been since the shooting, he suddenly felt optimistic that life was about to get better. And unlike Luka, he actually looked forward to paying a visit to Nevada City.

It would always be their hometown, and he still had a few friends there.

Ike's new attitude was offset by Luka's sense of dread. The thought of seeing Alannah caused his heart to quicken and he felt flushed. In the three years since he'd last seen her, he'd allowed himself to put that part of his life away in a place that he seldom revisited. On some days, his years with Alannah now felt more like a dream than a memory. He was pretty sure that seeing her again would rip that illusion all to hell.

Luka's dour expression caught Ike's attention.

"What's wrong with you? You look like I felt yesterday," Ike said.

"Ike, I don't know if I can face Alannah. I know I try to act like none of that matters anymore, but seeing her is going to feel like a cut with a knife," Luka said. He reached up and nervously rubbed his chin.

"I know it will, and I know what a sacrifice you're making for me. I wish I had some magical words that would make all your pain go away, but I don't. The older I get, the more I realize that some things are just not meant to be. You two tried to make it work for years, and have nothing to show for it."

Luka smiled. "Thanks, I guess. That wasn't the best speech I've ever heard you make."

"Probably not, but nothing I say is going to change how you feel."

"Be honest with me. Which one of us do you think was wrong? Was it me for not wanting to be a Catholic or her for insisting that I had to be? I was willing to let our children be Catholic," Luka said in exasperation.

Ike rubbed his lips with his fingers as he thought about how to answer the question. "On the surface, I'd say you were right. You certainly tried to compromise.

On the other hand, I don't think either one of us can appreciate the pressure she felt to please her family. They put her between a rock and a hard spot."

"I wasn't worth fighting for is what it all boils down to. Her parents never even tried to like me and she let it happen."

"Luka, you know better than me what a wonderful girl Alannah is. Every one of us has our weaknesses. Hers were such that they prevented your union, but you can't be bitter. You loved her for who she was, and that was part of her just as much as that great laugh she has."

Luka nodded his head. "You make a good point there, but I think I would have preferred you to tell me how stupid she was and that not marrying me was the biggest mistake of her life," he said with a snort.

"Oh, I know it was her loss. I just think her upbringing doomed her to a losing hand."

"Enough about this. Maybe I can avoid her the whole time we're in Nevada City. Damn, I swore I'd never go home, but here we go. I'll be fine."

Ike made a single nod of his head and didn't reply. He decided to save his speech on the folly of avoiding Alannah until they were home. A surge of love for his brother coursed through him, and he wished he had the power to mend Luka's broken heart. At that moment, Ike felt like the luckiest brother in the world. In spite of all the wounds this trip would rip open, Luka remained right there beside him to settle the score. "Sure you will," he said instead.

"With us headed back to Nevada City and all that's waiting for us there, I have to say that this feels like the trail to yesterday," Luka said.

"Yes, it does."

Chapter 20

Northern Colorado

Mackey McClure recuperated for a week at Dan and Dalilah's mountain cabin. His strength returned a little each day, aided by Dalilah's medicines and good cooking. He spent a good deal of time sleeping each day while taking an occasional walk to build up his endurance.

The brothers had formed a real friendship with Dan. The mountain man and Rusty would go hunting and fishing together on most days. Dan taught Rusty the finer details in the art of fishing for trout. After supper each evening, the three men would talk and play dominoes well into the night. Dalilah was a different matter altogether though. She seldom joined in any of the conversations, and she had a way of making Rusty uneasy with her penetrating stare.

After a breakfast of deer steak and eggs, Rusty retrieved two hundred dollars in gold coins from one of the bags of money the brothers had stolen from the freighters. "We stayed longer than I anticipated. I'm doubling what I promised you in the beginning," he said as he dropped the coins into Dan's hand.

Dan's eyes lit up and he smiled. "Thank you kindly. That's more than I usually earn in a year. You've put a lot of beans on the table for us," he said.

"It's a small price to pay for saving Mackey's life. We'll always be beholden to you and Dalilah."

"Well, you know where we live if you ever pass this way again."

"We'll do that."

As the brothers moved toward the door to leave, Dalilah said, "There's still time to change your ways before you both end up dead. If you don't, it's as sure to happen as the sun rising tomorrow morning."

The comment gave Mackey a chill and he failed to stymie a small shudder of his shoulders.

Rusty set his jaw and nodded his head. "Thanks again for saving my brother," he replied.

The brothers rode away out of the foothills to the North Platte River and started following it to the south. A cloudless sky allowed the bright sunlight to quickly burn off the fog along the river and take the morning chill out of the air. The day looked perfect for traveling.

Mackey let out a sigh. "I worried that you might kill Dan and Dalilah instead of paying them the money. Since we haven't had a chance to talk alone, I've fretted about that all week. You did the right thing," he said.

Rusty gave his brother a perturbed look. "And why would I do that? Dan is a fine fellow, and Dalilah saved your life even if she is one strange Indian. Sometimes I felt like she could read my mind."

"You didn't have any problems killing Ike's children is why. Sometimes you're not too particular on who you decide to kill."

"I'm not in the habit of killing people that I like or that do us a favor. You had me worried with that bullet wound. I was beginning to think you might not make it."

"Did you ever think about leaving me for the posse to find?"

Rusty stared straight ahead for a moment before speaking. "The thought did cross my mind, but you hung tough so I never had to worry much about it."

The answer didn't exactly reassure Mackey. It seemed to him that what his brother really said was that he would have left him if things had taken a turn for the worse. Mackey decided it was best to put the matter out of his mind. "Let's ride," he said as he spurred his horse into a fast trot.

The brothers rode all morning without stopping to rest. Mackey found that the riding didn't bother him at all, and the warm sun and fresh air were making him feel better than he had all week. He figured in a couple more days, he would be as good as new.

After Rusty and Mackey stopped at noon to water the horses and eat some jerky and hardtack, they wasted little time before resuming their travel. A couple of miles down the river, they came upon two men panning for gold on the riverbank. The prospectors stopped their work and warily turned to face the brothers.

"Are you getting rich?" Rusty called out good-naturedly.

"Naw, we just got here today. So far, we haven't found a thing," one of the men answered.

"Seems like a lot of hard work for little reward. I bet your back is aching by the end of the day."

"You get used to it after a while. We keep hoping we'll strike it rich, but it's beginning to look like this spot was a mistake."

"Yeah, I'd say you made a big mistake today," Rusty said with a laugh.

Rusty drew his revolver and started shooting. The first shot hit the man that had done the talking in the belly and he flopped to the ground. While he writhed in pain, the second man took off in a sprint across the river. Rusty emptied his Colt on the prospector, hitting him in the back. The shot severed the man's spine and he splashed headfirst into the river. Bubbles floated to the surface of the water as the man helplessly began to drown.

Mackey watched the whole thing unfold, too stunned to react. He sat speechless as Rusty calmly reloaded his gun and fired away until the man on the riverbank finally stopped jerking each time a bullet tore into his body.

"Why did you do that?" Mackey finally yelled.

"Because I didn't want you to think I was getting soft just because I didn't see fit to kill Dan and Dalilah this morning," Rusty replied.

"You killed two men just to prove a point to me? What in the hell is wrong with you? I never thought you were getting soft for a moment."

"Well, now you know for sure. I can kill anybody anytime the mood hits me."

"You're a crazy bastard, is what you are. Those men might have families that need feeding."

"I can kill them, but I can't bring them back to life, so quit lecturing me. Let's get to riding."

"I can't believe I left Calamity Jane behind to ride with you. We could have been happy together. You nearly got me killed and now you kill these poor boys just for the heck of it. I don't know what's gotten into you."

"Jane is just a drunk. She loves the bottle, not you. People will know the name Rusty McClure before my days are through. Just shut up and ride." Rusty nudged his horse into a walk.

Mackey let out a sigh and rubbed his forehead as he watched his brother riding away. He felt absolutely defeated and a little guilty for having ever mentioned the possibility of Rusty killing Dan and Dalilah. Rusty had done some wild and brutal things in his lifetime, but Mackey couldn't ever remember anything as unprovoked as what he'd just witnessed. He wondered if his brother could actually be crazy. The thought also crossed his mind that someday Rusty just might take a notion to kill him if the mood happened to strike him. He pressed his horse into moving. It wasn't as if he had any other options at the moment.

Chapter 21

Nevada City, Colorado

Ike and Luka arrived in Nevada City in the middle of the afternoon. As they rode past O'Sullivan's General Store, Ike could hear Luka breathing so rapidly that he sounded like a dog panting after a hard run. He glanced over at Luka and saw that his brother was staring straight ahead and looking as white as a sheet.

"Slow your breathing down and just relax. You're going to be fine," Ike counseled.

Luka took a big gulp of air and tried to tell himself to calm down. "Do you really think I can avoid Alannah the whole time we're here?" he asked.

Ike looked over at his brother again and grimaced in dread of what he was about to say. "Luka, I've been avoiding this conversation for as long as I possibly could, but I can't any longer. No, there is no way you can avoid Alannah. By suppertime tonight, you and I are going to be the talk of the town, especially since we're now wearing U.S. deputy marshal badges. You need to march into that store and say hello as if your visit was just as normal as any two friends catching up after a long time apart from each other. Otherwise, when you do cross paths with her out on the street – and you surely will – you're going to look weak and pathetic."

Luka flung his arm into the air. "Now is a fine time to be telling me this. You could have told me before now so I could think it over and prepare myself if I decided you knew what you were talking about."

"I know, but I didn't want you being miserable any longer than necessary."

"Oh, sure, I just love making quick decisions. You know how I am. I have to ponder everything to death. You don't mean I need to do it right now, do you?"

"I think you need to march into that store as soon as you gain your composure. Better she learns you're back from you instead of somebody else, and in this town, that'll be within the hour."

"I bet you're enjoying the hell out of seeing me act like some old lovestruck fool."

"Luka, I take no pleasure in any of this. I know how hard this is for you and that it stirs up all those old memories and feelings that you keep buried. You know I wouldn't have asked you back here if I thought there was any other way to find Rusty and Mackey."

"Oh, hell, I'm going to get this over with and put myself out of my misery. My heart's liable to give out if I don't shoot myself first."

Luka turned his horse and rode back toward the store.

Inside the shop, Alannah glided down the aisles as if she were floating. Mark Walsh had wasted no time in asking to see her again. They were going to go to dinner and then see a play that a traveling troupe would be performing that evening. She'd been giddy all day, and downright silly with the customers that came into the store. Most of her time had been consumed with trying to decide what she would wear that evening. Her parents were nearly as ecstatic as Alannah was over the sudden change in her fortunes concerning a suitor.

When Luka reached the store, he paused to grab the doorknob. He could feel his heart thumping furiously, and his chest felt so tight that he wasn't sure he could get enough air into his lungs to speak. The urge to bolt in retreat gripped him, but his feet wouldn't move. He cursed and loathed himself for being so weak over a woman he hadn't seen in years. Unable to bear the agony any longer, he grabbed the knob and barreled through the doorway.

The sound of the ringing of the bell above the door caused Alannah to look up from the cans she was stacking upon a shelf. Her mouth dropped open and her eyes grew as large as walnuts. She forgot to breathe, and loudly sucked in some air to banish the feeling that she was underwater needing to surface. The sight of Luka caused a rush of so many emotions that she felt overwhelmed, but the pang of love won out over everything else she felt.

"Hello – Alannah," Luka said in an unsteady voice.

"Luka, what on earth? What are you doing here? Hello," Alannah blurted out.

As Alannah stalked toward her old love, she spied the badge on his shirt. The surprising sight nearly caused her to stop in her tracks to ask about it, but instead she stretched to kiss his cheek.

"U.S. Marshal Tompkins hired Ike and me to clean up Nevada City."

Alannah looked up into Luka's blue eyes. She couldn't believe he was standing before her, and she wondered if her legs might buckle right out from under her. A part of her wanted to throw her arms around him and bury her head in his chest. Luka had an effect on her that apparently time would never erase. But another part of her wanted to hold him responsible for all that had gone wrong between them and knock his head off. She realized her greeting had been far from sounding welcoming. "I didn't mean to sound rude. It's good to see you again," she said a little stiffly.

"That's all right. I know I was about the last person you expected to see walking through that door."

"Actually, I'd say you were the absolute last person I expected. What about the ranch and the trading post up north? Did Irene and the children come with you?"

Luka had never told a lie to Alannah in his life, and he hadn't prepared himself for her interrogation. He stammered to reply. "Can we go somewhere private to talk?"

Alannah furrowed her brow and looked puzzled. "Sure," she said.

When they headed for the back of the store, Luka noticed Connor and Nora staring at him. He wasn't sure if their expressions were of shock or barely concealed disgust at his presence in their store. He gave a greeting as he passed by them. Alannah led him into the office and closed the door.

"What is it?" she asked.

"Alannah, I've never ever lied to you and I'm not going to start now, but you have to swear to me that you'll tell no one else what I'm about to tell you – not even your parents. Nobody else is going to know the whole story."

Alannah furrowed her brow again. She didn't like the sound of this. "You have my word. You know I never betray a trust."

"You better have a seat," Luka said. He waited for her to sit and then he sat down, too. "Rusty and Mackey tracked us down. I was away so they burned down our trading post. They killed Irene and the children. Ike nearly died from gunshot wounds. We're here to get them when they come home."

Alannah sat like a stone until her eyes started blinking rapidly as if she was waking from a coma. She let out a wail that caused the hairs on Luka's neck to stand on end. As she wept uncontrollably, he remained seated, watching her helplessly. He badly wanted to take her in his arms and make the pain go away, but he feared she would reject his efforts, and truth be told, he thought his heart might break for good if he once again held her.

When Alannah had finally cried herself out, she wiped the tears from her eyes and loudly blew her nose. "I wondered why Irene hadn't written me back. She always sends me a return letter as soon as she gets mine."

Stunned by the news that Alannah and Irene corresponded, Luka sat there pondering its ramifications. The women had always been friends in school, but the idea that they'd stayed in touch had never crossed his mind. If not for the delicate situation, he would have loved to ask what they wrote about in their letters. When Alannah had earlier mentioned the trading post, he'd wondered how she knew about it. He couldn't help but worry that Irene had written Alannah about how he never courted women anymore. The last thing in the world he wanted was for Alannah to think that she broke him. "I'm sorry to have to deliver such sad news, but we're here to kill Rusty and Mackey or take them back to hang them. What they did was worse than anything I ever saw in the war."

"Poor Ike, he must be devastated, and you, too. Irene always bragged on you for being so good to Little Ike and Marcy. I can't believe Irene is gone. We always talked of making plans of seeing each other again someday. I guess we waited too long and I'll never see them now."

"I wouldn't wish any of this on my worst enemy."

"Are you really going to clean up the town?"

"That is what the marshal wants us to do while we wait. I'm not sure how well all that will work. We're liable to have all you Irish trying to hang us," Luka said. He smiled to let her know he was joking.

"Some of us Irish like you two just fine, and a whole lot more know that this town needs a good cleaning."

"We'll see."

"Luka, it really is good to see you again. You look like you've taken fine care of yourself. I don't think you've changed a lick since you've been gone."

"I guess you probably sat around here and imagined me fat and bald by now. I would think that would be the easiest way to deal with the one that you let get away," Luka said in half-jest.

Alannah leaned back in her chair with an amused expression. She hadn't expected Luka to bring up the past, but his comment fired her up. "Who said I've been sitting around think about you? I have a gentleman calling on me tonight for your information. From what I heard, you're the one that has been sitting around pining over the past."

Luka set his jaw and grimaced slightly in a failed attempt not to show any reaction to Alannah's comment. Now he knew for sure that Irene had written Alannah about him. He would have paid twenty dollars to know if Irene had volunteered the information or if Alannah had asked about him. "I'm glad to hear that you are courting. I truly hope you find someone," he said.

Alannah recoiled like a cornered cat ready to attack. "Of course you do, that way you don't have to feel guilty that I wasted the best years of my life waiting for you to come to your senses."

Luka had no idea how to respond to her outburst. The couple stared at each other in silence until the quiet became uncomfortable.

"Well, I guess I better go," Luka finally said and stood. "Don't forget you gave me your word to keep all of this quiet."

Alannah stood and took Luka's hand. "Don't worry, I can keep a secret. And Luka, I'm truly sorry for the pain you and Ike are going through. Give him my condolences until I get the chance to do it for myself. The times that the four of us spent together were some of the best times of my life."

"You take care." Luka opened the door to leave.

"You too," Alannah called out.

After Luka was out of sight, Alannah closed the door and sat back down. She studied her palm that had held Luka's hand, and rubbed it with her fingers. The touch of his skin had felt like hot little sparks. She already regretted sassing him and mentioning her evening with Mark. Sometimes it was just so hard to let go of old bruised feelings. Her mind wandered to her friend, Irene. Alannah put her head down on the desk and began crying again. A day that had started with so much promise now felt like one of the worst days of her life. Not only had she lost a dear friend, but she also had to confront all those old confounding feelings she had for Luka. She had no idea what she would tell her parents about her tearstained face.

Luka stalked out of the store without bothering to tell Alannah's parents goodbye. He had to get out of there before he made a fool of himself. The urge to cry gripped him, and he cursed himself for bringing up the past with Alannah. Not only had he made himself look petty, but he'd also ended up on the short end of the exchange. Seeing her again proved every bit as bad as he feared it would be. She looked as pretty as ever, and still held a spell over him that time would never break. He found Ike waiting patiently on his horse down the street.

"How did it go?" Ike asked.

"It went fine," Luka answered a little too quickly. "She knows the truth, but she'll keep our secret. I couldn't lie to Alannah – I just couldn't."

"Slow down there. Are you all right?"

"I'm as good as I'm ever going to get. It wasn't any worse than ripping off a scab so you can watch yourself bleed."

"I'm sorry."

Luka shook his head and waved his hand through the air to make Ike stop taking pity on him. "Alannah sends her condolences. The news of Irene's and the children's deaths really hit her hard. She cried like a baby."

"Haven't we all?" Ike said in a quiet voice.

"So what is our next move?"

"We're going to the jail to make our presence known. I'm in the mood to rile up our fine City Marshal Grady Kelly."

The brothers rode their horses to the jail and tied them to the hitching rail they'd used hundreds of times before when they were the law in the town. They marched into the building as if they owned the place. Marshal Kelly and a deputy were standing at the stove, drinking coffee and shooting the bull.

The marshal looked toward the sound of the door closing. He did a double take when he saw the brothers. "Ike and Luka, what brings you back to . . ." He had spied the U.S. deputy marshal badges.

"Marshal Tompkins sent us here to keep an eye on the town. He's not happy over what's been going on here. We aim to put a stop to the lawlessness," Ike said.

Marshal Kelly spilled coffee when he slammed the cup down onto the stove. "What? He can't do that. I'm the city marshal and have say over my town."

"The U.S. Marshal's office can do pretty much whatever they want in their territory, and you know it. You had better just get used to us being here."

"I'll do no such thing. You two best watch yourselves."

Ike scratched his chin and grinned before speaking. "Marshal Tompkins gave us orders to throw your ass into your own jail if you give us trouble. I can't think of many things I'd take more pleasure in than that. You've been served notice, and you best heed it."

Grady puffed up his chest and pulled his shoulders back like a dog getting ready to defend its territory. "I guess things didn't work out so well in the Montana Territory and now you're crawling back to feed your family. You German boys won't be any more popular now than you were back in the old days."

The marshal's comments caused a rush of old bad feelings to come hurtling back to the surface. Ike balled his fists up so tightly that his knuckles turned white. He took a breath to try to calm himself for fear he'd lose control and give the marshal the whipping he deserved. "If we bring some law and order to this town, folks just might feel a little differently this time. Good to see you again." He turned and headed for the door.

When Ike and Luka were back outside, Luka asked, "What are we going to do for fun now?"

"I say we get a room at the hotel and a bath. I feel a little dirty after talking to Grady. That was kind of fun."

"Things are certainly going to get interesting around here."

Chapter 22

Nevada City, Colorado

Carter's Restaurant looked about half full to Alannah as Mark Walsh held the door open for her and she stepped into the business. She could feel every eye upon her and her new beau as they walked to their table. It seemed as if everyone in Nevada City had an interest in her love life, and she visualized the local newspaper running the headline 'Alannah O'Sullivan Spotted With A Man'. Mark helped her get seated in a chair, and while he took his seat, she looked around the room and stared into submission anyone that was still eyeing them.

"Are you all right?" Mark asked. "You seem a little distracted this evening."

Alannah forced a smile. "I'm fine, really," she said. "Today just didn't go as I planned. I guess it's weighed on me a little."

"Do you want to talk about it?"

"No, not really. I just want to enjoy the evening with you. I'll do better – I promise."

"Well, a good meal should get that started then."

While Mark and Alannah were looking at menus, Ike and Luka emerged from the hotel, freshly bathed and barbered. The brothers were hungry and in search of a good meal. Luka stepped into Carter's Restaurant and saw Alannah. He stopped so abruptly that Ike ran into the back of him. Before Luka had the chance to shove Ike back out the door, Alannah looked up and saw the brothers. Luka had no choice but to greet her with a single nod of his head.

Ike looked around the restaurant and saw what the problem was. "It's too late to run. Go straight to their table. I need to say hello to her anyway," he whispered.

Luka was in no position to argue with Ike. He let out a grunt and headed toward the table. "Alannah, it's good seeing you," he said.

Ike stopped beside his brother and reached over to put his hand on top of Alannah's hand. "Good to see you again. It has been awhile," he greeted.

"Good to see you two again, too," Alannah said. She mouthed the words "I'm so sorry for your loss" to Ike.

Ike forced a small smile and made a nod of his head to acknowledge the condolence.

Mark stood to shake the brothers' hands. "Gentlemen," he welcomed.

"I forgot my manners," Alannah said. "This is Mark Walsh. Mark, this is Ike and Luka Gunther."

After the handshakes were made, Ike said, "Well, we're hungry. We best get us a table before our bellies start growling. It's really good to see you again."

The four of them exchanged goodbyes, and Luka headed for the farthest table away from Mark and Alannah.

Mark sat back down and smiled. "So which one was it?"

"Which one was what?" Alannah asked in confusion.

"The beau that got away."

Alannah's face colored at the question. "It was Luka. They've been sent here by the U.S. marshal to bring some law to our town. The news kind of took me by surprise today, but I'm fine. All of that was a long time ago."

"I can see where it would put a bee in your bonnet. It's not every day that someone from your past just shows up."

"Can we please just talk about something else?"

"Sure. I probably should have just kept my mouth shut in the first place. Let's order our meals. We do have a play to catch after all," Mark said. His smile failed to hide some hurt feelings.

As soon as Ike sat down in his chair, he said, "I told you that you couldn't avoid Alannah. Aren't you glad that I made you go into the store earlier today? Think how awkward meeting Mark and her would have been if I hadn't."

Luka looked over at his brother in disbelief. He shook his head and rolled his eyes. "Really? After what I've been through today, you want to lecture me with the "I told you so" speech. I expected a little more support from you," he said.

Ike let out a little snort. "Yeah, you're right. I'm sorry. I know that none of this can be easy on you."

"You know, while I'm not going to lie and say seeing them together doesn't bother me, it isn't as bad as I thought it would be. Seeing Alannah today has brought up a lot of old feelings, but more than anything, it has reminded me that she and I were destined for failure. Mark seems like a good man. I hope she finds herself somebody that can be the person that I never could."

"Maybe so. Let's enjoy a good meal and then see if we can find us some trouble to get into later."

By the time the brothers finished stuffing themselves on beefsteaks, carrots, and stewed potatoes topped off with cherry pie, Alannah and Mark had left the restaurant. Ike paid for the meals and they took their leave to walk the streets of Nevada City.

"I wonder if Blood & Guts is still the worst saloon in town," Luka said.

"I was thinking about that myself. If Colin stills owns the joint, I would imagine that it's as wild as it ever was," Ike replied.

Back in the days when Ike and Luka were the law in town, the Blood & Guts Saloon proved to be a constant headache for the brothers. Gunfights, brawls, and assaults were commonplace occurrences. Colin McCoy didn't care what went on in his saloon as long as the money kept pouring in. The miners loved blowing off steam and spending their hard-earned dollars in the place. The Gunther brothers and Colin had their fair share of run-ins, but the saloonkeeper always managed to just barely stay on the right side of the law.

"If we're going to get things back to how they were when we ran things, I'd say the Blood & Guts would be as good a place to start as any," Luka said.

"I suppose you're right. I don't know why we bothered to bathe if we're going in there," Ike complained. "I kind of like the smell of hair tonic. That'll be gone by the time we leave that dump."

"Lead the way."

Ike and Luka walked down the street and into the Blood & Guts. The place was even dirtier and louder than Luka remembered. A cloud of smoke hung like a fog and helped alleviate the smell of body odor and spilt beer. Miners were crowded around the tables and the bar, laughing and shouting at each other to be heard above the din. Heads began to turn toward the door as the customers caught sight of Ike and Luka wearing their new U.S. Deputy Marshal badges. Colin stood behind the bar, and when he saw the brothers, he paused in drying a glass.

"Colin," Ike greeted. "We'll have beers."

"I heard a rumor that you two were back. I could hardly believe it. You're about the last two I ever thought I'd see again," Colin said.

"Same here. I can't say that you've gotten any prettier," Ike said.

Colin grinned before going to get the beers. When he returned with the drinks, he asked, "So are you really here to clean up the town?"

"Word always did travel fast in Nevada City. That is why we're here. We figured we'd start in the worst place."

"You and Luka always could manage to ruin a good party."

Ike took a sip of beer to let the comment linger. "We try our best," he said.

The brothers stood at the bar and drank beers. Occasionally, one of the townsfolk would come up and greet Ike and Luka, but the conversations never got past exchanging pleasantries. The town might have been ready for some law and order, but that didn't mean they were any more willing to like the Gunther brothers.

An hour later, a fight broke out over a game of poker. A miner flung himself over the table and tackled another miner. The men crashed to the floor and began pummeling each other as the crowd cheered them on.

Ike and Luka drew their revolvers and moved toward the disturbance as if they hadn't missed a beat in the years since they were the town's lawmen. The miners had already bloodied each other up with their fists and teeth. Just as Ike and Luka parted the crowd to get to the men, one of the miners pulled his knife. Ike cracked the knife-wielder over the head with the barrel of his Colt. The blow knocked the miner to the floor in an unconscious heap.

Luka pointed his revolver at the nose of the other man and cocked the gun. "I'm going to blow your nose for you if you do anything silly. Understand?" he threatened.

The miner nodded his head.

"Some of you carry this man to the jail," Ike ordered. He looked toward the other brawler. "You're coming too."

A couple of men hoisted up the unconscious miner while Ike and Luka marched the second man down the street. Inside the jail, they found a lone deputy playing solitaire.

"We need to lock these men in separate cells," Ike said.

"Marshal Kelly isn't going to like that," the deputy said.

"I don't care what he likes. Either do it, or I will, and I'll throw you in there with them, too."

The deputy scowled, but retrieved the keys from his desk and walked toward the cells.

After the men were locked up, Ike said, "You can tell whoever is here in the morning that they can let them go. Just make sure they know that these two were trying to kill each other."

"I guess I'm your messenger, too."

"You're probably better at that than you are a deputy."

The brothers returned to the Blood & Guts. They were greeted with hard stares from Colin and the customers. It seemed the crowd didn't approve of the interruption of a good fight on a Thursday night.

"Two more beers," Luka said.

"We're not the only saloon in town that has plenty of fights. Don't you boys need to make the rounds?" Colin asked.

"Oh, we will in due time, but tonight you're the lucky winner of having U.S. deputy marshals on hand for your protection needs. You should feel honored and very safe," Luka said.

A few minutes later, a whore came running down the stairs, bawling at the top of her lungs. She was dressed in only her pantaloons and camisole. Her lips were busted and her nose bled.

"What's wrong with you?" Colin hollered.

The whore had to quiet her crying and catch her breath before she spoke. "My john wanted to do something that I ain't letting no man do and he hit me because of it," she cried out.

All of the miners broke out into fits of laughter and catcalling.

"As long as a customer is paying, he can do whatever the hell he wants. Now get your ass back up there," Colin yelled.

The whore's face scrunched up like a child being scolded. She turned and started stomping back upstairs.

"Stop right there," Luka hollered.

Nothing got Luka's ire up more than a man hitting a woman. It was something that he just wouldn't tolerate. Back in the day, he and Ike had tried to get a law passed in the town to make prostitution illegal, but got nowhere with their plan – too much money in too many hands for that to have ever happened. He'd always had a soft spot for the whores and tried to look out for them, but even then, some of the girls had ended up in a bad way.

"Mind your own business. This doesn't concern you," Colin complained.

"Assault is against the law," Luka said as he marched past the bar and up the stairs.

The place got as quiet as a congregation waiting for Sunday service to begin. The silence didn't last long. Upstairs, it sounded as if a war had erupted. Glass shattered on the floor and the breaking of furniture and bodies crashing made it seem as if the ceiling was about to come down upon all of them. A man tumbled down the stairs wearing only his long johns. Luka strolled closely behind him. He grabbed the bloodied man by the underwear and began dragging him out of the saloon.

Luka paused at the bar. "I'm going to come back tomorrow and check on that girl. If you so much as look at her wrong, we're closing this place down for an inspection. Do you understand?"

"You damn Germans never . . ."

Colin dropped to the floor, silenced by Ike's fist punching him in the mouth.

"Let me help you," Ike said as he grabbed an arm of the man Luka was dragging.

Once they were outside, Luka said, "Welcome back to Nevada City. If we weren't the talk of the town by this afternoon, we will be by tomorrow morning."

"We're just doing what we were sent here to do. We never won any popularity contests in the old days, and we won't start now."

"I don't miss any of this. I was quite content to hang up my guns and run the store."

"I know you were. We'll get back there as soon as we settle the score, though you do make one hell of a lawman."

Chapter 23

Nevada City, Colorado

With Luka's shocking return to Nevada City, Alannah found herself on the losing end of a battle with sleep. She even avoided going to bed because she knew she'd be tossing and turning for hours before rest would come. If she wasn't crying over the deaths of Irene and the children, she was thinking about Luka and all the conflicting emotions he caused her to feel. The one thing she allowed herself to admit was that Luka still had a powerful hold over her. When he walked unannounced into the store that day, the sight of him had made her feel as giddy as the first time he told her he loved her. As she lay sprawled out in her bed trying to get to sleep, she even managed to giggle as she visualized herself as a candle melting right before his very eyes. But love had never been her and Luka's problem, and what had been their problem, would always be their problem.

Also adding to her troubles was the unfortunate timing of Luka's return and Mark Walsh coming into her life. After the awkward start to the evening when Ike and Luka showed up at the restaurant, she and Mark had enjoyed a wonderful evening at the play. They had laughed throughout Shakespeare's *A Midsummer Night's Dream*. The one thing that Mark had over Luka was their shared love of plays and poetry. Mark was a sophisticated man. On the other hand, Mark had never – or at least not yet – caused her to wake up from a dream so sensual that she had felt herself blush in the dark.

In the morning, Alannah dragged herself out of bed and went to the store. Between her drowsiness and all that occupied her mind, she found work to be a difficult thing on which to concentrate. When the clock struck ten o'clock, she told her mother she had some errands to run. She headed for Clancy's with the hope that Betty Anne and Wanda were out of bed. With all that had been going on, she hadn't had the chance to tell the girls about Mark or of Luka's return. Alannah slipped into the back of Clancy's and found Wanda and Betty Anne sitting in their nightgowns, drinking coffee and smoking cigarettes.

"Well, look at what the cat dragged in. We thought with your new beau and Luka back in town that your love life must be too busy for us saloon girls," Wanda teased.

"You know about all that?" Alannah asked incredulously.

Betty Anne giggled. "There aren't many Lukas in the world so we figured it had to be him, and you and Mark Walsh are the talk of the town. For some reason, everyone around here has always been fascinated with the last remaining Miss O'Sullivan. This is Nevada City after all."

Alannah poured herself a cup of coffee and took a seat. "You girls take the fun out of everything," she said.

Wanda snickered. "You look like hell. Pleasing two men must be hard work. I'll say one thing though – you sure know how to pick them. Those are two good-looking fellows."

The comments affronted Alannah. She stood to leave. "I'm glad you find this all so amusing. I needed someone to talk to, but I don't need this."

Betty Anne reached across the table and snagged Alannah's wrist. "Sit back down. You know that Wanda gets her mouth in front of her brain sometimes. She didn't mean anything. Talk to us. She'll be good."

Alannah looked skeptically at Wanda as she sat back down.

"I'll be good. You must be stressed. You've never been offended when I've teased you before," Wanda said.

"I guess I am, and I'm tired. I'm having a hard time sleeping, too."

"Tell us everything," Betty Anne said.

"Mark has been coming around to the store a lot, and the other day he asked me to go for a walk and dinner. We really had a nice time. In fact, he's the first man since Luka that has actually piqued my interest. He's a Catholic and so smart. We have a lot in common. In fact, I have more in common with him than I do Luka. We were all set to go to dinner and the play the other night, when Luka shows up out of nowhere. Girls, I'm just going to be honest with you – seeing him again made my knees go weak. I don't know why his return is bothering me so much. Nothing has changed between us. We will never find a compromise that will work for both of us, so what's the point? It's just that Luka has a powerful hold on me, and I know for a fact that he doesn't even try to court girls anymore. I'm not looking for any answers from you two, but I just needed to vent some out loud."

The saloon girls looked at each other, waiting for the other to speak first.

Wanda cleared her throat. "I think you've already answered your own questions. If you and Luka haven't figured it out by now, you never will. You need to let him go and see if Mark is the one for you. He sounds pretty tempting."

Betty Anne smiled, not surprised that she and Wanda would have different points of view. "I don't know. There is nothing in this world that will ever replace the first one that you fall in love with. That's something that will still be special to you on the day you die. At this point in your life, does it really matter what your folks think about who you marry? Your happiness is the important thing."

Fighting the urge to cry, Alannah's bottom lip protruded. She leaned back in her chair and looked at the girls. "I know a thirty-year-old woman should be able to do what she wants and not worry what anyone else thinks, but I can't. I'm just not made that way," she said.

"Well, there's your answer then," Betty Anne said. "You need to get with Luka and just talk things over. Bring a close to all of this so that you both can get on with your lives."

"But we've done all that before, and look where it's gotten us. I fall to pieces seeing him, and he doesn't even try to find someone else."

"You might have closed the door, but you certainly have never locked it. If there is no room for compromise, then stop torturing yourself. Let him go."

Alannah took a sip of coffee and let the silence hang for a moment as she pondered what Betty Anne had said. "You're right. I already knew all of this, but I needed to hear you say it. I'm going to talk to Luka to ease my mind and push him to get on with his life, too."

"You're strong and you'll be fine," Wanda said.

"I sure hope so. I have to get back to the store."

Alannah jumped up from her seat and returned to the shop.

Just after lunchtime, Luka came into O'Sullivan's to buy some salve. He was sporting a black eye, and his knuckles were skinned and raw.

"What happened to you?" Alannah asked.

"We've been breaking up fights right and left. I was bound to take a punch sooner or later. Nobody has died since we've come to town. One miner got stabbed the other night and he's in pretty bad shape. I need some salve for my knuckles," Luka replied.

Alannah fetched a tin of salve and handed it to Luka. "You need to be careful," she warned.

"I'm trying. It's certainly no fun taking a fist to the face. By the way, I'm sorry we chose the same restaurant the other night. I certainly didn't mean for that to happen." He fished some money out of his pocket and paid for his purchase.

"It was fine. At least I got to see Ike. Luka, we need to go somewhere and talk. I need to say some things."

Luka furrowed his forehead and tilted up his head. "Sure. When do you want to do it?"

"Let's just do it now and get it over with," Alannah said. She turned so that she could see her father over by the pickle barrel. "I need to leave with Luka."

"That will be fine," Connor said, though the tone of his voice said otherwise.

The brusqueness of the reply struck Luka wrong. In all the years he had courted Alannah, he had never once confronted the O'Sullivans over their distaste for him. He wasn't a boy any longer and he'd had enough of it. With a heavy sigh, he strolled over to Connor. "Mr.

O'Sullivan, in all the years I courted Alannah, I always treated her with the respect she deserves. I fought for my country and I helped make this town a safer place to live. Most families would be happy to have me join them. You have kept two people apart that would have had a wonderful life together all because I have German ancestry and I'm not Catholic. You should be ashamed of yourself. I hope you are happy."

Connor's face turned red and his face contorted in anger. "I know what is best for my daughter. You have no children and cannot understand," he shouted.

"And thanks to you, I never will." Luka turned and headed for the door.

Alannah followed Luka outside. "Why did you do that? You didn't accomplish anything by making Daddy mad."

"Yes, I did. I got the satisfaction of finally telling him how I felt."

"I suppose, but I'll probably be the one that suffers for your actions. Let's walk to the pines where we used to sneak off to."

"Let's go," Luka said. He managed to let go of his anger enough to smile.

The day was warm and sunny with just enough breeze to keep the air feeling fresh and invigorating. Alannah and Luka talked little as they strolled to the edge of town where the pines grew on the sides of the foothills. They disappeared into the trees and sat down in the pine needles.

"So what do we need to talk about?" Luka asked.

Alannah started fidgeting with her hair the way she always did when she felt nervous. She let out a sigh before inhaling a breath as she worked up her resolve. "Luka, I will love you until the day I die, but nothing has changed between us. You saw how Daddy was today. They will never accept you into the family. I know this probably makes me a weak person, but it's just the way it is. I just wanted to get this all out in the open."

Luka squeezed his lips together and slowly nodded his head as he pondered what she had said. "Why did you think I thought otherwise?"

Pulling her head back, Alannah looked at Luka and frowned. "Because of that remark you made the other day about me letting you get away."

"I am the one you let get away, and you just said you'd love me forever. That sounds like you let the right man get away to me. Listen, I didn't harbor any illusions that my sudden return here would change your mind. You're right in that nothing has changed. What your family thinks will always be more important to you than me – that's just the way it is, I came to terms with that when we quit seeing each other, but we'll always be special to each other. Let's just make the best of the situation until I head back to Bozeman. I never thought I'd be back here again and I hope it will be true this time."

"All right then, I guess we agree on most things except where you said that what my family thinks is more important than you. It's just that what they think would have never allowed us to be happy together. There would have been too much tension."

Luka shook his head in dismay. "Whatever you say. We've had this conversation more times than I can count and I hope to never have it again. For the record, Mark seems like a fine man. I hope he turns out to be the one for you. You deserve to be happy and have a family."

Alannah puffed up and cut her eyes toward Luka. "Of course you do. Only the noble Luka Gunther could wish that the girl he loves would be happy with another man. I can't believe you would speak those words. Honestly, some of the things you say."

"Good God, Alannah, you are confusing. What good would it do if I was jealous? I've never understood jealousy. It doesn't accomplish a thing. I guess you'd be happier if I cried and begged you to take me back. I won't do such a thing. I will leave here with my honor intact. We need to move on with our lives."

"Well, I'd be jealous if the tables were turned. If you really love someone, I don't see how you could wish them happiness with another person. Maybe you don't love me that much. And you haven't moved on with your life. You just stopped in your tracks."

Luka let out a chuckle. "God, I'll never understand women. They should come with a manual."

He leaned over and kissed Alannah hard on the mouth. She didn't resist him. Luka kept kissing her until they were both aroused and then he abruptly stopped. "I just wanted to give you something to compare to when you get around to kissing Mark. See if he can make the sparks fly like I can." Luka jumped up and stalked off out of sight.

Alannah wanted to be mad, but the truth of the matter was that Luka had stirred her up too much even to try to go there. It had been so long since they'd kissed that she'd forgotten how wonderful the intimacy between them was. In his arrogance, Luka had certainly been right that the sparks had flown. She felt so warm that she could imagine their passions had set her dress on fire.

Chapter 24

Nevada City, Colorado

The McClure brothers made it to the outskirts of Nevada City without any further mayhem. They'd been on the trail every night since they'd left Dan and Dalilah's place except for an evening spent in Eastom, Colorado, where they'd spent the night playing poker and had sold their two extra horses to the blacksmith there.

After Rusty had killed the two prospectors, Mackey decided he would part ways with his brother if such a thing ever happened again. Killing people when necessary was one thing, but cold-blooded murder for no reason whatsoever was something else altogether. He informed his brother of his intentions. The threat seemed to work. A couple of situations presented opportunities for Rusty to cause trouble, but he'd ridden on without so much as a second look.

"I think we should take the backway to Ma's place just in case the law is looking for us. Ma will have heard if trouble is brewing," Mackey said.

"That's probably a good idea. I still don't think we have to worry about Luka or the law, but it's best to be cautious," Rusty replied.

The brothers pulled their hats down low and avoided the busier streets of town as they traveled to their mother's small cottage. As they rode, Rusty and Mackey avoided eye contact with the few people they encountered along the way. Once there, they hid their horses in the small two-stall barn behind the house before knocking on the door.

Miss McClure let out a squeal when she saw her sons. She reached up with both her hands and rubbed the cheeks of her sons before welcoming them into her home. "I've been worried sick about you two. You should have written me. I thought you'd come straight home as soon as you were released from prison," she said.

"We had some things we needed to do first," Rusty said.

Miss McClure eyed Rusty suspiciously but didn't ask any questions. "Let's go sit at the table and get caught up. I'll put on a fresh pot of coffee."

"How have you been, Ma?" Mackey asked.

"I've been fine. Money is tight like always, but now that you boys are home, things will be better. The mine is hiring. You two can get you honest jobs now and make something of yourselves. In time, people will forget about what you did here." Miss McClure pumped water into the coffee pot and lit the kindling in the stove.

"So what's new in Nevada City?" Rusty asked after his ma sat down to wait for the coffee to brew.

"Nothing much changes around here. The miners still get up and go to work each day and go to the saloons each night to start a ruckus. Well, there is one thing that's new. And I'm telling you two right now that you need to let bygones be bygones. They didn't have no choice but to arrest you two for what you did. Ike and Luka Gunther are U.S. deputy marshals sent here to clean up what our city marshal doesn't see fit to do," Miss McClure said.

"What?" Rusty hollered. "That can't be."

Rusty and Mackey exchanged glances. The expressions on their faces looked as if they'd just seen a ghost.

"Well, it is. I saw them with my own two eyes. In fact, they spoke to me and were as nice as they could be. Luka said he hoped you boys came home so he could give you a proper greeting."

Mackey looked down at his lap and started rubbing his forehead.

Rusty turned pale. "If this don't beat all," he mumbled.

Miss McClure studied her two sons. She'd seen them in trouble on enough occasions to know the signs. "What did you do this time?" she asked.

"We didn't do nothing," Rusty said.

"Rusty, tell me what you did. I might be old, but I'm not a fool, and I've seen that look enough times before now to know trouble when I see it."

Rusty yanked off his hat and threw it to the floor. "We went to the Montana Territory and shot Ike. I could have sworn he was dead. Luka was gone or we would have killed him, too."

"And we killed Ike's family," Mackey added

"Shut up," Rusty yelled.

Miss McClure let out a shriek before covering her mouth. Tears ran down her cheeks and she began sobbing. When she could speak, she said, "How could you do that for being sent to prison for something that you did? You have no idea what you've done. I guess I should have told you years ago, but I gave my word. You tried . . ." She stopped and gulped air as she tried to find the will to continue speaking.

"What is it, Ma?" Mackey coaxed.

"You tried to kill your own brother. All you boys have the same daddy," Miss McClure blurted out.

"What?" Rusty screamed. "That can't be. Are you sure?"

"Of course I'm sure. He was the only man I've ever known. Gustave Gunther was your father. Look at Mackey. He looks more like Ike and Luka than he does you. I always feared someone would figure it out by looking at him. I kept my secret so I wouldn't ruin Gustave's life, but I should have told you boys after he and his wife died."

Rusty and Mackey sat in silence. Both were too numb to speak. Not only were they in grave danger, but they'd just been upended by the most shocking news of their life.

The coffee boiled over, and Miss McClure went to the stove and dumped a little water out of the pot.

"So all these years of hating those damn Germans, and now I find out that I'm half of one," Rusty muttered.

"Yes, you are. That's why I always told you to not judge them for their ancestry."

"I'm a damn half German."

Once Miss McClure had calmed from her initial shock, she started to anger. She turned toward her sons and shook her finger at them. "You are far worse than that. How could you kill a woman and her babies? I must have failed you both in your raising. That is pure evil, and I fear for your souls."

"I'm not worried about our souls, but our lives is another matter altogether. Ike is not one to take lightly," Rusty said.

"I'll walk with you to the jail. They won't gun you down in front of me. You have to give yourselves up."

"Ma, they'll hang us if we surrender. There isn't a judge in the whole country that wouldn't sentence us to hang after what we did to Irene and those two children. We have to run."

Silence hung in the air again until Miss McClure asked, "Mackey, you've been awfully quiet. What do you have to say?"

"I'm sorry, Ma. You didn't fail us. We were raised better than what we did. It all seems so wrong now. I guess I knew it as soon as we did it. And I still can't fathom that we're brothers to Ike and Luka. We couldn't be more different," Mackey replied.

"That's because you never had a father to keep you straight and lay down the law. Lord knows, I tried, but you boys were too much for me to keep in line. That's a failing I'll regretfully take to my grave," Miss McClure lamented.

"No wonder their pa always stared at us. He was looking at his own flesh and blood," Rusty said. He looked up at his mother with tears in his eyes. Finding out that his father was Gustave Gunther had turned his world upside down to the point that he couldn't even concentrate on Ike and Luka being in town.

"I say we head out at nightfall," Mackey said. "We have some money to give to you before we go. You won't have to worry anymore about paying bills."

"And where did this money come from?"

"It doesn't matter. What's important is that you don't have to do without necessities any longer," Mackey said.

Miss McClure didn't respond. She went to the stove and poured three cups of coffee that she set down on the table. "Let's have some coffee," she said.

Mackey dutifully took a sip before speaking. "Rusty, what are you thinking?" he asked.

Rusty looked over at his brother as if he'd just been awakened from a nap. "We need to find Ike and Luka, and kill them. Luka never worried me, but Ike's a different matter altogether. After the things we did to his family and him, we'll be looking over our shoulders for the rest of our lives if we don't end this now. I won't live that way."

"They are U.S. deputy marshals," Miss McClure reminded her sons. "You can't kill them. Every law officer in the country will be after you if you do such a thing."

"We'll have to make our way to Mexico. The law won't follow us there," Rusty said.

Miss McClure started to cry again. "This is terrible. Brothers against their brothers. It's like Cain and Abel all over again. Your souls will be lost to Hell for sure and you'll spend the rest of your life wandering in the land of Nod."

Mackey jumped up and began pacing around the kitchen. "Rusty is right. We need to end this now. I always knew we didn't take this seriously enough. Luka would have been here waiting for us even if we'd killed Ike. Now we'll have to face both of them."

"It's settled then," Rusty said. "We'll leave all the money here with Ma in case things don't go as planned. We can come back to get some of it and say our goodbyes afterward. I'm not worried about Marshal Kelly or his deputies pursuing us. They wouldn't mind seeing the Gunther boys gunned down."

Miss McClure plopped her arms onto the table and buried her face in them. The sound of her weeping filled the kitchen and caused her sons to look away from their mother. "I beg you not to kill again," she blubbered.

Chapter 25

Nevada City, Colorado

As the Gunther brothers were eating lunch at a small restaurant called Sam's Eatery, Luka decided he was going to burst if he didn't tell Ike about his encounter with Alannah the previous day. He'd played the event over in his head so many times that he needed to talk about it before he went crazy.

"I had to go into O'Sullivan's yesterday to get some salve for my knuckles. While I'm there, Alannah tells me we need to talk, so we sneak off into the pines like a couple of teenagers. She informs me that nothing has changed between us. I couldn't believe it. You would have thought that I came back here just to beg her for her hand in marriage or something. I don't know what's gotten into her," Luka said.

The sudden outburst caught Ike by surprise, and he glanced up at his now loquacious brother. He tried to hide his dismay that he'd have to listen to the saga of Luka and Alannah for maybe the thousandth time. He hurriedly chewed his bite of sandwich and swallowed it down. "What did you say?" he asked.

"I told her I agreed. And then get this – I told her that Mark seemed like a good man and that I hoped he was the one for her, and she got all offended. I couldn't believe it. I'll never understand women."

Ike let out a chuckle. "You two never change. If you spent as much time practicing making babies as you did fighting, you'd have a whole army of brats by now. And you'd be too tired to fight."

"Well, good luck with that. The honorable Miss Alannah O'Sullivan will die a spinster before she ever consummates her love without a ring on her finger. From years of experience, I can promise you that."

Shaking his head, Ike said, "So I guess you two aren't speaking now."

Luka smiled mischievously. "I put a kiss on her that curled her toes – I could tell. Then I stalked off to leave her to think about that for a while. I don't know if she's mad or not, but whatever she is, she can't deny that I can make her purr like a kitten."

"Oh my. So much wasted time that neither of you can ever get back. I'd give anything for one more day with Irene and the kids. On most days, I beat myself up about all the time I spent trying to make the ranch perfect while I should have been home spending that time with my family. That will haunt me all the way to my grave."

"I know it does, Ike. I wish there was something I could do or say that would make things better, but it just doesn't work that way, does it?"

"No, it doesn't, and I'm not sure time will be the great healer that some claim it to be. Surely it will get some better though. I'd hate to think I'm going to feel this bad forever."

"I hope time helps you some. I wonder when Rusty and Mackey will show up," Luka said, hoping to change the subject.

"I don't know, but I hope it's sooner than later. I'm ready to get back. We aren't going to make any difference here that will last. As soon as we're gone, things will go right back to the way they were."

"I suspect you are right."

"Let's walk down to the jail. I want to make sure the papers were filed for the grand jury to review on that miner that stabbed the other man. Marshal Kelly might see to it that they get lost. I heard the miner is a friend of his."

Luka paid the bill and they walked to the jail. The only law officer back from lunch was Deputy Milt Harris. He had been a deputy for Ike back in the day, and had been the one that Ike had telegraphed to find out that Miss McClure was still living.

"Hey, boys," Milt greeted.

"Hey, Milt," Ike said. "I wanted to make sure the grand jury got to see the case against that miner that stabbed that man."

"I made sure the papers were filed before Grady got ahold of them. We still have him locked up."

"Good. Glad to hear that. You always were a good deputy for me," Ike said.

Milt smiled. "You boys had best watch your backs. I went home for lunch, and my wife told me that she saw Rusty and Mackey riding toward their ma's place. She said they wouldn't even look her way as if they didn't want anybody to recognize them. Those boys won't be thrilled to know you two are back in town."

Luka glanced over at Ike. His brother's face had lost all expression as if he was in a stupor.

"That's certainly good to know," Luka said.

The comment snapped Ike out of his reverie. "Milt, we're here to arrest them. They killed my wife and children. Stay in here even if you hear gunfire. This is personal. Luka and I are going to handle this."

"Sure, Ike, whatever you say. I'm so sorry for your loss. I never had much use for Rusty and Mackey, but I never thought they'd stoop that low," Milt said.

Ike nodded his head before looking over at Luka. "I guess we're about to find what we came looking for."

Luka gulped a breath of air and nodded his head. "It seems so. Feels like we've been chasing them for years."

Ike squeezed his lips tightly together and returned the nod. He had to fight off getting overwhelmed with emotion. "I wouldn't be here without you. You're the best brother a man could have. I truly appreciate all you've done for me."

"I wouldn't have it any other way. You'd have done the exact same thing for me."

"Are you ready?"

"Let's get this over with. Just be careful."

"You too."

Ike and Luka paused at the door to look each other in the eye. They extended their hands for a final shake before they cautiously stepped out of the jail and scanned the town. They spotted Rusty and Mackey tying up their horses across the street a half block down in front of Fitzgerald's Dry Goods Store. The McClure brothers also saw the Gunthers. They drew their revolvers and started shooting. The first shots slammed into the jail and forced Ike and Luka to dive behind a water trough for cover while bedlam erupted as the noontime crowd on the boardwalks scurried for safety.

"This isn't the way I envisioned this playing out," Luka said.

"Me either, but it is what it is," Ike replied.

The Gunther brothers exchanged gunfire with the McClures. A shot hit Rusty's horse in the hip. The horse began bucking wildly while still tethered to the hitching rail and caused the other horse to dance out of danger's way. In the chaos, Rusty and Mackey fled into Fitzgerald's store.

Mr. Fitzgerald and all the other old codgers that loitered there nearly fell over themselves getting out of the way of the brothers.

"Mr. Fitzgerald, I know you keep a scattergun behind the counter. Don't you dare touch it or I'll have to kill you," Rusty warned.

Fitzgerald raised his hands above the counter so that they were in plain sight.

"What do we do?" Mackey asked.

"We wait for them to come through that door and blow them to hell," Rusty answered.

Ike and Luka reloaded their revolvers and emerged from behind the water trough.

"I'll go around and come in through the back. You give me some time before you come in the front. All right?" Ike asked.

"Anything to get this over with," Luka replied.

Ike took off at a sprint down the side street and then cut into the alley behind the store while Luka moved cautiously toward the front of Fitzgerald's. Once Luka felt sure that Ike had arrived at the back of the store, he began creeping past the front of the shop to reach the door.

The McClure brothers were squatted down in an aisle, waiting for something to happen. Rusty saw Luka sneaking by the window. He stood up and fired, shattering the glass. The shot missed, but a shard cut through Luka's shirt and slashed his arm. Luka turned and began shooting into the store, causing Rusty and Mackey to scramble to another aisle.

Mackey looked up and saw Mr. Fitzgerald point the shotgun their way. He tackled his brother to the ground as the blast sent chunks of crockery flying through the air.

"Let's get the hell out of here," Rusty hollered.

The brothers sprinted for the back of the store just as Ike swung the rear door open. Ike saw Rusty and Mackey barreling toward him with their guns pointed his way. He dove off the landing and scrambled behind some packing crates as the brothers bolted out the door.

Ike popped up above the wooden box he was using for cover and fired. His shot hit Mackey in the thigh, causing the outlaw to fall as his leg buckled. Rusty spun toward Ike and kept him pinned down with gunfire as he helped Mackey to his feet. They moved toward the next building where they took refuge in the City Restaurant. Women screamed and men jumped to their feet at the sight of the brothers barging into the rear of the building.

"Everybody get down on the ground," Rusty yelled. He fired his last bullet to drive home his point.

"Can you stand?" Rusty asked.

"I think so," Mackey replied.

"Good. Get your gun reloaded."

Mackey tested his leg and found he could still stand. The brothers raced to reload their guns before their next encounter with the Gunthers.

"You stand right here, and as soon as that back door opens, start firing. You surely can't miss Ike at that distance. I'll go to the front to get Luka," Rusty said.

"Be careful."

"You do the same."

Mackey stationed himself with his gun cocked and aimed at the back door. Rusty moved toward the front of the restaurant and took a position at the end of the counter.

Outside the back door of the restaurant, Ike cocked his Colt. He wasn't about to make the same mistake twice. Taking a breath to steady himself, Ike vowed to avenge the deaths of his family. He flung the door open and fired as soon as Mackey came into view. Mackey fired at the same time. The two men stood a mere ten feet apart, firing as quickly as they could cock their guns and pull the triggers. Both men winced as bullets tore into their bodies. Mackey took two bullets to the chest. A third bullet to the face killed him instantly and he dropped to the floor. Ike suffered three gunshots to his chest. He staggered into the restaurant. "Luka, finish what we started," he whispered and fell dead on top of Mackey.

Luka heard all the commotion and ran in front of the restaurant. Rusty fired at him, shattering another window. He and Luka exchanged gunfire much as their brothers just had, but from a greater distance. Luka hit Rusty in the left arm. Rusty cursed and ran for the rear of the store, passing the bodies of Mackey and Ike.

"Ike," Luka called out.

A voice from inside the restaurant meekly hollered, "I think your brother and Mackey are dead."

Luka looked up toward the heavens before vowing to kill Rusty. If he'd had time, he would have sat down and cried, but instead, he ran to get a view down the next side street, fearing that Rusty would cross it and go into O'Sullivan's to kill Alannah just for spite. The street was deserted. As he reloaded, he wondered what course of action he should take.

Rusty had turned in the opposite direction and ran to the livery stable. He pointed his gun at the blacksmith.

"Saddle me up the best horse you have in this barn and do it quick," he ordered.

The blacksmith never said a word, but jumped into action. He pulled a horse from a stall and quickly bridled and saddled the animal.

"Much obliged," Rusty said.

Rusty mounted the horse and dashed out of the barn. He turned back toward where all the fighting had taken place. Standing in the middle of the street was Luka.

Luka felt calm as he watched Rusty racing his way. He didn't care if he lived or died as long as Rusty died with him. That was all that mattered now. He had to avenge all of his family's deaths if he had any hope of his soul finding peace. Luka raised his Colt and waited for Rusty to come into range.

"You are going to die," Rusty bellowed with his first shot.

The two men fired upon each other as they neared one another. Luka hit Rusty twice in the abdomen. Rusty put a shot into Luka's chest just before falling from the horse and bouncing hard upon the street. Luka's wound knocked him onto his back and his revolver went flying through the air.

"Luka, you've killed mé, but I'm going to kill you before I die," Rusty yelled as he slowly got to his feet.

Luka was having trouble breathing. He struggled to crawl toward his gun.

Rusty started moving toward Luka. The pain of his wounds caused him to walk stooped over and he used his hand to support his shot up stomach. "I learned some interesting news today from Ma. You're going to love this. Mackey and me are Gustave Gunther's bastard children. We're all brothers." Rusty paused to laugh at the absurdity of the news. "Ain't that something? I wonder what old Gustave would think of all his sons dying on the same day. Maybe we'll all end up in Hell together in the same room. Wouldn't that be fitting? We could torture each other for eternity."

Luka desperately tried to reach his gun, but was still a few feet from his Colt when Rusty stopped and raised his pistol. For a brief moment, Luka and Rusty stared into each other's eyes. The sound of Rusty cocking his revolver was obliterated by the roar of both barrels of a shotgun. The buckshot slammed into Rusty's chest and sent him staggering backwards a couple of steps. He looked toward the source of the shot, and through the cloud of gun smoke, he saw Alannah still staring down the gun barrels at him. She was the last thing he ever saw.

Alannah threw the gun down and ran to Luka. She pulled him over onto his back and cradled his head. His chest wound made a sucking sound and blood frothed around his mouth. She instinctively covered the gunshot with her hand to make the noise stop.

"Somebody get a doctor," she screamed.

Connor O'Sullivan appeared in the store's doorway. He took one look at his daughter and Luka, and ran for the doctor's office.

Alannah started to weep. She didn't have a free hand to wipe away the tears and could barely see Luka for the stinging in her eyes. "Luka, don't you dare die on me now. I can't bear to lose you. I don't care anymore if you're a Lutheran, Catholic, or even an atheist. It all seems so silly now. I promise I'll marry you, but you have to live for me."

Luka mouthed the words, "I love you."

"I love you, too." Alannah leaned over and kissed his forehead.

Dr. Hardy and Connor jogged up to Alannah and Luka. They bent over and braced their hands on their knees as they tried to catch their breaths before either of them could talk.

"His chest is sucking air," Alannah said.

The doctor nodded his head. "We need to carry him on a hard surface," he said before gasping for another breath. "It needs to be wide enough that you can straddle him to keep pressure on the wound but narrow enough to get through my doorway."

Connor didn't speak, but again took off at a jog.

"This is bad, isn't it?" Alannah asked.

Dr. Hardy made eye contact with Luka before answering. The young man looked alert and didn't seem to be in shock. "It is, but he's got a chance if we can seal the wound before too much air gets into his chest. You are keeping him alive right now. Did you get to see if there was an exit wound?"

"There was. I saw it when I rolled Luka onto his back."

A crowd had begun to gather around them to gawk, and Connor had to maneuver through the people to get back to Luka. He carried the top of a packing crate. The lid was five feet long and about two feet wide.

"That'll do," the doctor said. "Alannah, keep pressure on the wound. Some of you men that are just standing here need to help me get Luka onto the board."

As the men lifted Luka onto the crate lid, he let out a groan and lifted his head in pain. Alannah managed to keep the injury covered during the transfer. She scampered over Luka and straddled his waist as she continued to keep pressure on the gunshot wound. The four men lifted the makeshift stretcher and began the trek to the doctor's office.

Luka managed a smile. He whispered, "I've been dreaming of seeing you like this since I was a teenager."

The humor in such a dire situation gave Alannah a moment of respite. The tension she felt gave way, and she broke into a fit of giggles. For the first time, she thought Luka just might live. After years of trying to be what everyone else wanted her to be, she no longer cared what anyone thought or heard. "You get well and I'll give you a dream a whole lot better than this," she said with a wink at Luka.

After the men maneuvered through the doctor's doorway, Alannah climbed off the lid. As they lifted Luka onto the exam table, she continued to cover the wound. The men departed while the doctor scrubbed his hands. He methodically retrieved all the supplies and instruments he would need to treat Luka.

"All right, remove your hands," Dr. Hardy instructed.

Alannah lifted her hands, and the doctor grabbed the shirt and ripped it open. He rapidly washed away the blood around the wound with soapy water.

"Look at the bullet hole in Luka's shirt and tell me if it tore open or if there is a chunk of material missing."

Alannah lifted the shirt and used her fingers to move the torn material back into place. "This old shirt is so thin that it just gave way. It's all here. For once, it served Mr. Gunther well to be cheap about his clothing."

"Good. That's one less thing to worry ourselves over."

Dr. Hardy doused the wound with iodine before he began threading a needle with suture. "Luka, I'm going to have to sew your wound shut. I don't want to put you to sleep. It's just too dangerous. All right?"

"Do what you have to do," Luka whispered.

As the doctor sewed the wound shut, Luka kept his eyes locked with Alannah's dark eyes. He gritted his teeth together, but showed no other signs of the pain he was enduring. When the doctor had the wound stitched shut, he placed linen squares over the injury and applied drops of collodion to seal them tight.

"One side completed," Dr. Hardy said when he applied the last piece of linen. "We'll wait a few minutes for that to dry and then we need to roll you over and start all over again. Luka, how does your breathing feel?"

"Better," Luka whispered. "Elephant off my chest."

"Good. I don't think the exit wound is taking in air. The muscles are probably sealing it off, but we have to seal it to be safe."

After a few minutes, the doctor and Alannah helped Luka roll onto his stomach. Luka let out a groan as he got into place. Dr. Hardy repeated the same steps on the rear wound until he had completed the task. When the collodion had dried, they helped Luka back onto his back.

The doctor then scrubbed the cut on Luka's arm from the broken glass. He finished with a dousing of iodine. "I may sew this arm up later, but it's fine for now. We'll see if it closes on its own."

As the doctor washed the blood from his hands, he said, "Luka, I believe in being honest with my patients. I'd say you have about a fifty percent chance of living. You've made it through the worst part, but things could still go wrong. If the wounds don't fester, I think you'll be able to take this young lady dancing."

"Thank you, Doc," Luka said.

"My pleasure."

"Yes, thank you, Dr. Hardy," Alannah said.

The doctor retrieved a blanket and a pillow for Luka. "I'm going to give you two a few minutes and then he needs to rest to regain his strength."

Alannah straightened her posture and looked at the doctor. "I'm staying with Luka. I won't get in the way or bother him, but I will not leave his side," she said.

The doctor smiled at her feistiness. "Very well," he said before heading toward the back of his office.

"You saved my life," Luka said.

"It was my only chance to marry in this lifetime," Alannah joked.

Luka smiled before turning serious. "I believe Ike is dead." He paused and his eyes filled with tears. "You need to have the undertaker embalm him and pack his coffin with salt or charcoal . . ." Luka stopped to inhale in order to have enough wind to continue. "I promised Ike that if he died I would bury him beside Irene."

"I'll go do that as soon as you fall asleep."

Luka eyes were drooping. They were nearly closed when they shot wide open. "If I die, will you hire somebody to take us back? Have them bury me on the other side of Ike. Bring me a bank note . . ."

"No, we're not even going to discuss you dying. Death is off the table. Luka, I meant what I told you. I will not waste another day of my life, and I won't have my life dictated by what my parents think any longer. Seeing you almost die in the street has given me a whole new perspective on life. If you'll have me, I will marry you. I love you so much."

"Of course I'll have you. That's all I've ever wanted. I love you, too. Always have and always will."

Chapter 26

Nevada City, Colorado

When Alannah walked into the funeral parlor to talk to the undertaker, she was unprepared to see the bloody bodies of Ike, Rusty, and Mackey all stretched out on tables. Her legs started trembling and she had to stiffen them to hide her condition. The memories of days spent with Luka, Ike, and Irene came rushing back again. With a deep breath, she fought off the urge to cry so that she could matter-of-factly tell the undertaker of Luka's wishes for Ike's body.

The sight of Rusty's shot up corpse caused Alannah to confront the fact that she had killed another human being. She didn't feel guilty for what she'd done – Luka would be dead for sure if she hadn't – but she wished she'd never been put in such a position. Killing another person was about the last thing in the world that she ever imagined she would do. She knew the memory would haunt her for the rest of her life.

On her walk back from the funeral parlor, Alannah slowed her pace. She needed to get her mind around all that had happened. It felt as if more things had taken place that day than had transpired in all the previous days of her entire life. As she neared the doctor's office, she saw Marshal Kelly walking down the boardwalk.

"Alannah, I need to speak to you for a moment," the marshal called out.

Alannah stopped at Dr. Hardy's door and waited. "What is it?" she asked impatiently.

"I understand that you were the one that gunned down Rusty McClure today. Is that true?"

"I prevented Rusty from killing an unarmed officer of the law."

"Luka?"

"Yes, Luka."

"Couldn't you have warned him to drop his gun before you blew him to pieces?"

"He knew he was already dying – he even said so. I don't think anything would have stopped Rusty from killing Luka besides me killing him. I would think you would be happy that a citizen defended a U.S. deputy marshal. You certainly were nowhere to be found."

Marshal Kelly bristled at the comment. "I don't think Luka being a deputy marshal had anything to do with it. It looks to me as if two sets of brothers that always hated each other finally decided to settle their grudges."

"Rusty and Mackey killed Irene and their two children. Ike nearly died from his wounds. They were here to arrest the McClures for those murders."

"First I've heard anything about this."

"Maybe if you spent more time at your job and less in the saloons you would know what's going on."

"Some might say you murdered Rusty to save your beau."

Alannah tapped her foot in agitation. "Marshal Kelly, if you can get a grand jury to take me to trial, I'll gladly face a jury of my peers. No one would ever convict me of saving Luka's life, and the town would laugh you out of a job. So think about that before you threaten me."

"All you O'Sullivans think you're a little bit better than everybody else around here, don't you?"

"No, we just think we're a little bit better than the likes of you. I don't have any more time for this nonsense."

The marshal took a step toward the door. "I need to hear Luka's side of the story."

"You are not going to bother him today. He's resting and very ill."

"You can't stop me. I'm the marshal of this here town."

"If you take one more step, I'll scream my bloody head off. I'm sure that the town already thinks you are a coward after today. What will they think if you accost a defenseless woman?"

Marshal Kelly turned and stalked off without saying another word.

Alannah went into the office and found the doctor sitting beside the sleeping Luka.

"How's our patient?" she asked.

"He was in a lot of pain. I had to give him a dose of laudanum to get him comfortable. He's resting better now," Dr. Hardy answered.

"He hasn't worsened, has he?"

"No, not at all. He's doing better than could be expected. Luka is going to have some rough days before things get better."

Dr. Hardy stood. "Have a seat. You're going to be doing a lot of sitting now. I have some books if you'd like to read to pass the time."

"Maybe later, but thank you for the offer."

The mention of books got Alannah to thinking about Mark Walsh. She dreaded the conversation that she would have to have with him. The murders of Ike's family in the Montana Territory and all that followed in its aftermath had probably changed the course of both

Mark's and her life, but she had no regrets over the decision she'd made. Now more than ever, she knew she wanted to spend the rest of her days with Luka. She reached over and took his hand.

By early afternoon, Alannah was getting hungry and her butt felt numb from the hard chair. She would occasionally stand and move about the office, but not stray far from Luka's side. Dr. Hardy had administered as much laudanum as he dared, but Luka would grow restless about every twenty minutes or so. Sometimes he was confused, and at other times, he seemed to be on the verge of trying to get out of bed. The doctor was busy with other patients in the adjoining room so Alannah didn't dare leave for food.

Mrs. O'Sullivan arrived at the doctor's office carrying a basket.

"Momma, what are you doing here?" Alannah asked.

"I figured you were getting hungry and I wanted to see how Luka was doing," Nora responded.

"I am hungry. I think all the chaos must do that to you. Luka is doing as well as can be expected. Dr. Hardy thinks he has a good chance to recover."

Nora reached into her basket and retrieved a sandwich that she handed to her daughter. "Good. I'm glad to hear that. I also wanted to tell you how brave I thought you were today. You risked your life to save Luka. Your father and I stood there helplessly while you went into action. That is love."

Alannah smiled sheepishly. "Thank you, Momma. I really appreciate you saying those things." She bit off a chunk of sandwich like a dog attacking a steak.

"Goodness, Alannah, don't get choked and keep your fingers out of the way. I wouldn't want to see you bite one of them off."

Alannah got tickled and had to cover her mouth for fear that food would spew out. Some humor was just what she needed after such a trying day. When she got the bite swallowed, she said, "Momma, I'm going to marry him."

"I know you are, honey. You're a grown woman and capable of making your own choices."

"Daddy will never approve of me marrying Luka."

"Well, Connor will have to decide whether losing a daughter or adding a Protestant to the family is the lesser of the two evils. I've already made up my mind."

"You were always as bad as Daddy as far as Luka was concerned. Why the change?"

Nora looked down at the floor and scratched the back of her neck. "You know, I'm not really sure. I might be getting older, but I guess I'm not so set in my ways that I can't change an opinion once in a while. I think it started when Luka showed up out of the blue in the store the other day, and I could see that no matter how much you two had been through together, you still had that spark. I've been feeling guilty for my role in keeping you two apart ever since then. Back when you and Luka were kids, I always thought you'd find somebody else, but that just never happened. I thought Mark was finally going to be the one for you, but some things are just meant to be and some aren't. Today proved to be the last straw in my resistance. I'm prattling like an old woman. Just know that you have my blessing."

Alannah reached out and hugged her mother. "Thank you. That means the world to me."

"Finish your sandwich. You'll need your strength to take care of your man."

The mother and daughter continued talking while Alannah finished the sandwich. As she ate a cookie that her mother had retrieved from the basket, Luka began to stir. He let out a groan and opened his eyes.

"Mrs. O'Sullivan," Luka said in surprise.

"I brought Alannah some food to eat. I'll be going now. Luka, I'm glad you're recovering. You need to get well," Nora said. She patted Luka's leg and gave Alannah a kiss on the cheek before leaving.

With a solemn expression, Luka looked over at Alannah. "When I opened my eyes and saw your mother, I thought for a moment that I'd died and gone to Hell."

Alannah broke into a fit of giggles that caused her to snort for air. "Shame on you. For your information, my mother just gave me her blessing for us to marry." She leaned over Luka to stroke his hair. His eyes were glassy and looked pained, and the corners of his mouth fought a battle to defeat a grimace.

"If this is what it took, I guess I should have gotten shot to pieces about twelve years ago."

Alannah reached over and took Luka's hand. "That gunshot wound is letting the wit just ooze right out of you."

"It's the medicine. I feel funny."

"You are funny. You woke up a couple of times and were confused. I thought you might try to get out of bed."

"Believe me when I say that I know I've been shot and that Ike is dead. I wish I was confused about that."

"I know you do. Just get some rest, and I'll go get you some food in a little while."

Alannah watched as Luka's eyes slowly sank shut.

Chapter 27

Nevada City, Colorado

For the first couple of days after the shootings, Luka spent most of his time sleeping. Whenever he was awake, Alannah plied him with broth and eggs. Dr. Hardy dosed him with laudanum whenever the pain became too much, and changed the bandages twice a day. During the long hours, Alannah constantly stayed by Luka's side except to sleep or to get food for them. The doctor had been kind enough to set up a cot for her when she became too weary to sit in the chair.

On the fourth day, Luka felt well enough to sit up in bed. He remained in a lot of pain, but he refused the laudanum when Dr. Hardy offered him a dose. Luka hated the way the medicine made his head feel and he made the decision to do without it. His color still looked ashen but better than the day before, and he remained dark under the eyes. He made an effort to smile as much as the throbbing in his chest allowed.

Luka got lost in thought as he stared off into space.

"Are you missing Ike?" Alannah asked.

The question brought Luka out of his reverie and he looked over at Alannah, surprised she had noticed his pondering. "Sure, I'm missing him, but I was thinking about what Rusty said just before he was going to kill me. Did you hear what he said?"

"I did."

"Do you think he told the truth?"

Alannah tilted her head and pursed her lips as she contemplated how to respond. "I've thought about that a lot while you've slept. I have to think he was. He was dying and ready to kill you. As much as he hated you and Ike, I don't know why he would have claimed you were his brothers unless it were true. And besides, I don't think Rusty had the imagination to come up with that on his own."

"Yeah, that's kind of what I've been thinking."

"Luka, as hard as that news is to bear, it doesn't change who your father was to you. He might have made a mistake, but he was still a good man. You can't change the past or what he did."

"I know, but it sure is hard to get my head around. I wonder if my momma knew. That had to be crushing to her if she did. She deserved better than that. I'm going to have to talk to Miss McClure when I'm better."

"I can't imagine how that can go well, but you're right that you need to talk to her. I'll go with you if you like."

Luka gave a sad smile. "Why don't you get out of here for a while? Go have yourself a bath and relax. I'll be fine, and you need a break. That old hard chair is going to ruin the shape of your butt."

Alannah cocked her head and peered at Luka. "I'm not sure how to respond to any of that. Are you trying to tell me I'm getting stinky? And I'm not sure whether I should be flattered or worried about your concern about my derriere."

"Oh Lord." Luka shook his head. "Don't overthink it. Just go and do something besides worry about me. I'm going to be fine."

As Alannah stood, she bent and gave Luka a lingering kiss on the lips. "Very well. I'll see you later. Once I have me a bath, I think I'll run a couple of errands."

Alannah hadn't been gone ten minutes when Marshal Kelly strutted into the doctor's office. He marched over to Luka and sat down in the chair that Alannah usually occupied. "I need to interview you," he said.

Luka smiled. Alannah had already told him about having run off the marshal on the day of the shooting, though she hadn't felt the need to inform him of the lawman's threat to prosecute her for shooting Rusty. "I noticed you waited for Alannah to leave before you showed up. I guess she put the fear into you."

Grady Kelly puffed up and pulled back his shoulders. "So I understand that you lied to me. Your purpose for being here was to kill the McClure brothers."

"No, you have that all wrong. We were here to clean up your mess and arrest Rusty and Mackey. They started shooting at us as soon as we walked out of the jailhouse. It's hard to arrest men when they are trying to kill you. Contact Marshal Tompkins if you don't believe me."

"I just might do that. I don't appreciate him sending you here in the first place."

"Marshal Tompkins read an account of what happened in the newspaper. He sent me a telegram with his condolences and thanking me for ending the McClures' lives of crime. He even said he planned to put Alannah up for a commendation. You can read it if you want."

"Alannah better worry more about getting charged with murder. She shot Rusty in cold blood."

Luka gave a contemptuous smile. "Yeah, you try that and see what it gets you."

"Is that a threat?"

"No, that's a promise. She saved my life while you were hiding behind your momma's skirt. This town will take you down if you mess with Alannah. And if they won't, Marshal Tompkins or I will."

Marshal Kelly jumped up from his seat and stalked out of the office, leaving Luka in a triumphant mood. The last thing that Luka feared at this point in his life was the likes of Grady Kelly. He closed his eyes and allowed himself the pleasure of imagining Alannah's and his wedding night.

After Alannah had departed from the doctor's office, she went home and began heating water for a bath. When she had enough hot water, she stripped down, grabbed her book of William Blake poems, and crawled into the tub. The book of poetry made her think of Mark, but she quickly banished him from her mind. She just wanted to relax in the hot water and not think about anything stressful for a little while.

By the time the water turned tepid, Alannah felt so calm that she had to fight off the urge to crawl into her bed for a nap. She resolved to get a couple of difficult conversations out of the way before she returned to the doctor's office. After dithering on what to wear, she chose her red dress. The outfit went well with her skin tone and dark hair. She hoped Luka would think she looked fetching in it.

Since it was Saturday, she thought she might find Mark at home. She had never been to his house, but she knew where he lived. On the walk there, she didn't allow herself even to think on what she would say to him. If she did, she knew she would just make herself a nervous wreck. When she marched up to his door, she didn't even hesitate before knocking.

Mark opened the door and reared back his head in surprise. "Alannah, I wasn't expecting you. I hear you've been quite busy."

"Hi, Mark. Can we talk?" Alannah asked.

"Sure, come on in."

Alannah followed Mark into the home and took a seat beside him on the sofa. She glanced around the room to get a sense of how Mark liked to arrange his home. The room looked impeccably clean and organized, and left no doubt that it had been furnished by a man.

"So, I guess you heard about me killing Rusty McClure and that I've been sitting with Luka," Alannah began.

Mark nodded his head. "I have. I stopped into the store. Your mother filled me in on all that had happened. Of course, the gunfight was already the talk of the town so I already knew about that part of it."

"I don't know how to go about this but to just go ahead and say what needs saying. Mark, you're a wonderful man, and truth be told, you and I are probably more compatible than Luka and I will ever be. I think if the timing would have been better, that you and I could have had something special, but when Rusty was about ready to kill Luka, two things kept racing through my mind. One was that I had to save Luka, and the other was that I had wasted a lot of years that should have been spent with him. I can't continue to make that mistake any longer. I'm sorry, but Luka has had my heart since I was a girl."

Mark squeezed his lips together and gave a half-hearted smile. "I understand completely. I wish you and Luka the best. I truly do."

"I hope in time that you can forgive me."

"There is nothing here that requires forgiving. Like they say – the heart wants what the heart wants. I just showed up in Nevada City a little too late for my own good."

Alannah leaned over and kissed Mark's cheek. "I hope you find your special one. In my heart, I believe that you will."

"Goodbye, Alannah."

"Goodbye."

Once Alannah was out the door, she let out a sigh of relief. Her talk with Mark had gone better than she could have ever imagined. Mark Walsh was definitely a classy man in a town where men of that ilk were in short supply. With one conversation down and one to go, she headed for the store to talk to her father. That was the talk that she really dreaded.

O'Sullivan's General Store bustled with Saturday shoppers. Alannah pitched in with helping customers in the hope the store would clear out and she could talk to her father. Thirty minutes went by before the last of the patrons left the shop.

"Daddy, I need to talk to you," Alannah announced.

Connor solemnly nodded his head. His wife had already informed him of his daughter's decision concerning Luka. Ever since then, he'd carried on an internal battle regarding how he should handle the situation without ever reaching a conclusion. "Let's go to the office," he said.

Alannah dutifully followed her father to the office and took a seat. After Connor softly closed the door, he sat down behind his desk. Tension hung in the air as they looked at each other, waiting for someone to speak.

"Daddy, I'm going to marry Luka. If anything good has come from what's happened, it's that I know I will not live any more of my life without him. Even if he wants to go back to the Montana Territory, I'll go with him. You know he's a good man. It would mean the world to me if you would accept him into the family," Alannah said.

An awkward silence followed as Connor rubbed a finger across his lips. "Alannah, you know how I feel about marrying outside of our faith, but you are a grown woman and I will not interfere with what you want."

"But will you give us your blessing?"

Connor turned his head and stared down at his desk as he rocked back and forth in the chair. "I don't know that I can do that. That's a hard thing for me to swallow."

"Would you have married Momma if she had been a Protestant?"

The question caused Connor to lean back and rub his chin. "That's hard to say since I always knew she was Catholic. I doubt I would have ever tried to court her if she wasn't. That's where I made a mistake with you. I should have run Luka off the first time he showed up at my doorstep, and then none of this would be a problem now."

"But you didn't, and Daddy, I love him with all my heart. I've always known that. Now I know I can't live without him."

"Just do what you have to do. That's the most I can offer now. It's more than I ever thought I would concede."

Alannah fought off the urge to cry. Her daddy had given in more than she expected, but not as much as she'd hoped he would. She wanted his blessing in the worst of ways. "Thank you," she said.

"Tell Luka that I hope he recovers quickly. I do want you to know how proud I am of you for what you did. That was a brave thing that you did for Luka."

The compliment embarrassed Alannah, and she grinned sheepishly. "I figured I had to save my last chance at getting a man," she joked.

Connor smiled for the first time. "Oh, by the way, have you heard any of this nonsense going around town that Marshal Kelly might try to get you charged with murder?"

"He threatened me, but I'm not worried about that. This town would never convict me for saving a lawman's life even if he is a Gunther."

"You let me take care of this. I'll have a word with Father Mulder. He'll get a stop put to it."

"Thank you, Daddy." Alannah stood and walked around the desk where she kissed her father on top of his head. "See you soon."

On the walk back to the doctor's office, Alannah felt as if her relaxing bath was all for naught. The stress of the talks with Mark and her daddy had caused her shoulders and neck to tighten up. Even though the conversations had gone better than she feared they might, they had robbed her of every ounce of fortitude she possessed. If not for it being a busy Saturday for saloons, she would have snuck into the back of Clancy's for a beer.

Inside Dr. Hardy's office, Alannah was flabbergasted to find Wanda and Betty Anne sitting on either side of Luka's bed. Both women were laughing and having a good time. Dr. Hardy sat at the foot of the bed. He and Luka seemed to be enjoying themselves just fine, too. All four of them were drinking glasses of beer. For the first time in a long, long time, Alannah felt a pang of jealousy.

"How did you girls get away from the saloon on a Saturday?" Alannah asked in voice filled with bewilderment.

"We just told Clancy that we were going to be gone for an hour while we came to see you whether he liked it or not. He didn't have much choice in the matter," Betty Anne answered. She retrieved a glass and the beer pail, and deftly poured a drink that she handed to Alannah.

"I see you've made some new friends since I left Nevada City," Luka said. He arched his eyebrows and smirked.

Alannah took a long drink from her glass before replying. The beer tasted good and proved to be just what she needed to relax again. "Yes, I have. Wanda and Betty Anne are two of the finest friends a girl could have. They've commiserated with me many a time – usually about a hardheaded man that moved to the Montana Territory."

"I'll drink to that," Luka said. He held his glass in the air to toast the others.

Chapter 28

Nevada City, Colorado

On Monday morning, Luka and Alannah had just finished eating a breakfast of ham and eggs that she had bought at the City Restaurant. Luka, feeling the best he had since getting shot, had devoured the food. He was growing restless from all the bedrest, and was anxious for Dr. Hardy to return from a call so that the doctor could change the badges and tell him if he could start doing a little walking.

The rusty-hinged outside door screeched open. Luka and Alannah glanced up expecting to see the doctor, but instead saw Miss McClure walk into the office. The sight of the woman caused Luka's breath to catch in his throat. He could feel his heart begin to race, and he glanced over at Alannah. She looked as shocked as he felt.

Miss McClure walked directly to the foot of Luka's bed. She looked at Alannah and then toward Luka. "I think we probably should talk if that is all right with you," she said.

"I would like that," Luka replied.

"First off, I want you to know how sorry I am that you lost Ike and his family. I don't know where I went wrong with Rusty and Mackey. They never were saints, but I didn't think they were murderers. I tried my best with those boys."

"I know that you did and I'm sorry it had to come to all of this, but they had to be brought to justice for their crimes. What they did was just awful."

"I know. You deserve to know the truth about everything. God only knows how many people have asked me about what Rusty told you before Alannah saved your life. Can you imagine the audacity of those folks coming right up to me to ask me to my face? I'm sure you have some questions."

Luka took a deep breath and hesitated to speak. As much as he wanted to know the truth, he dreaded what he might hear. "Did we really all share the same pa?"

Miss McClure nodded her head. "You did. I'll just tell you the whole story so that you don't feel as if you have to pry the information out of me. Ike was a colicky baby. He took all of your mother's attention. I think Gustave felt neglected. What we did was so wrong. I'll not make any excuses for either of us. He started calling on me after he left the saloons at night. The whole thing ended shortly after I realized I was with child – twins. I wasn't about to ruin one family to make a new one so I agreed to keep our secret. Over the years, Gustave would slip me some money whenever he had a little extra. He was a good man, but not perfect – just like all of us. I hope this doesn't change your opinion of your father. I'll regret till the day I die that I didn't tell Rusty and Mackey the truth after your parents were gone. I might have spared us all this grief that's never going to end."

"Did my . . . did my momma know the truth?" Luka asked in a soft voice.

"No, I don't believe she ever suspected a thing. I was around her enough that I'm sure I would have picked up on her feelings toward me if she had known, and I never got that impression at all."

"Thank God for that."

"Yes, I agree," Miss McClure said before her thoughts drifted back to her sons. "I never understood why Rusty hated you boys so much. I never talked down about your family or about Germans either. He came up with all that on his own and nothing I ever said could change things."

"Maybe on some level he knew the truth deep down inside."

"Maybe. Luka, I hope you recover and have a good life. I don't bear anyone any ill will for what has happened. That goes for you, too, Alannah. Nothing that Rusty and Mackey could ever do would have changed my love for my boys, but they brought this upon themselves. I'll blame myself for the way they turned out until the day I die."

"Thank you, Miss McClure."

Miss McClure looked to be on the verge of tears. She flipped her hand up for quick wave goodbye before darting out of the office.

"Are you going to be all right?" Alannah asked.

Luka rubbed both of his hands through his hair. "I guess I'll have to be. I certainly can't change what has happened, but I'll tell you, it's a tall order to get my head around the fact that my pa did such a thing and that Rusty and Mackey were my brothers. I would have never suspected Pa to be capable of doing that to Momma in a million years."

"I know. None of us ever wants to see the fallible side of our parents. Right now, you are dealing with more than any one man should have to bear at one time. Just know that I'm here for you if you want to talk."

"I don't know what I'd do if I didn't have you right now – I sure don't have anyone else. I'm not sure life would be worth living."

Dr. Hardy finally returned to his office in the late morning. He had delivered a baby that had taken its sweet time in coming into the world. The doctor looked tired and grumpy as he went about cleaning his instruments.

"Let's have a look at you," Dr. Hardy said brusquely as he turned toward Luka.

The doctor removed Luka's bandages and examined the wounds before grabbing his stethoscope to listen to the heart and lungs. When he finished, he gently removed the instrument from his ears and set it down on the bed. "The wounds don't need bandages any longer. The air will do them good. Just be sure to keep them clean. Today is the first day that I didn't hear any noise in your lungs. You are a lucky man to have lived through this. You can thank Alannah and me for keeping you alive. Don't tire yourself out. Your lungs do not need to be strained right now. The wound could tear open if you do. You are free to go. My buggy is outside. I'll take you to wherever you want to go since I don't think you'll be up to walking far."

Luka and Alannah looked at each other in surprise. Neither had thought the doctor would let Luka leave just yet. They had made no plans for when he did.

"You can just come and stay at my home," Alannah said. "There is no point in staying at the hotel. I'm going to be by your side one way or the other, and I'd rather do it at my place than there."

"Don't you think that will cause a bit of a scandal?" Luka asked.

"Honestly, at this point, I don't think one more scandal in Nevada City will make a bit of difference. People can think what they want. Let's go. I'm ready to sleep in my own bed."

Luka turned toward the doctor. "I don't know how I can ever repay you for all that you've done for me. I'm much beholden to you."

"Money will do nicely," Dr. Hardy said. As soon as the doctor spoke, he realized that in his weariness he had sounded flippant. "I shouldn't have said that. You were certainly a challenge and I'm just thankful that I proved up for the task. It's been my honor to be your doctor."

Luka smiled. "I'd be tired of having me in your office, too, if I were you. I'm just as ready to leave as you are to have me gone. Thanks again."

The clock in the doctor's office struck twelve o'clock as Luka walked slowly out of the building with Dr. Hardy and Alannah by his side. As Luka gingerly hoisted himself into the buggy, he glanced up the street and saw a large crowd standing in front of the jail. "I wonder what in darnation that is all about," he mused.

"Well, let's go see," Dr. Hardy said as he and Alannah crowded into the carriage.

The doctor turned his buggy around in the street and headed toward the crowd. As they got closer, they could see Marshal Kelly and a couple of his deputies step out of the jail. Father Mulder and Connor O'Sullivan were facing the lawmen with what appeared to be most of the Catholic congregation at their backs.

Marshal Kelly raised his arms to quiet the crowd. "All of you just need to go home. You have no reason to get yourselves all worked up," he hollered.

Father Mulder took a step forward. The sun reflecting off his white hair made it appear as if his head was a beacon of light, and from his years of preaching, he had a voice that boomed like a thunderbolt. "We understand that you are going to pressure a grand jury to bring charges against Alannah O'Sullivan for murder. This town should be giving that woman a parade for all she has done to save a lawman's life. If that wasn't justifiable homicide, I don't know what it was. What do you have to say for yourself?"

The marshal rubbed the back of his neck and had a hard time looking directly at the Father. "I'm just trying to get all the facts before I write my final report. I took an oath to uphold the law."

"Grady Kelly, I've known you since you were a baby. Don't you mess with me. If you or any other Catholic has a hand in bringing charges against Alannah, I'll excommunicate every last one of you. And I'll see to it that you are banned from every business in this town that is owned by a Catholic, including those saloons that you spend most of your time in when you should be protecting this town. Do I make myself clear?" Father Mulder bellowed.

"Yes, Father Mulder, I understand completely."

"Good. You had better not forget what I told you. Thank you everyone for lending your support. Have a blessed day."

As the crowd began to disperse, Luka turned toward Alannah and grinned. "Your daddy might not have any use for me, but he sure does love you."

Alannah blushed. "I told you that he wished you a quick recovery the other day. That's a start."

Dr. Hardy turned the buggy around and drove to Alannah's house. After Luka thanked the doctor one more time, the couple walked into the home.

Luka looked around the front room and grinned. "So this is what the home of a single, wanton woman looks like. I bet you, Wanda, and Betty Anne have you some wild times in here."

Alannah put her hands on her hips and straightened her posture. "Luka Gunther, just because you about died on me doesn't mean you can say whatever you want any more than it ever has. You best watch your tongue."

Luka snickered and wrapped his arms around Alannah. He planted a kiss on her lips that he imagined was curling her toes. "I love you more than I ever have," he said when he ended the kiss.

"I love you, too, but calm yourself. This wanton woman of yours doesn't want to be the reason that you die on the spot. I've been known to have that kind of power over men," Alannah said with a devilish grin.

"God knows I've waited enough years to find out."

"You're not the only one that's waited. I've saved myself for my wedding night. I highly doubt that you can say the same thing."

Luka's face colored, but he didn't respond to the accusation. "I need to sit down."

Alannah let the moment pass. "I need to go talk to Mrs. Blake. She is going to have a conniption fit when she finds out you are staying here."

"I remember her. She was mean before she got old. I hate to imagine what she's like now."

"That's right. You can thank me later. I'm also going to the hotel to settle your account and have them send your and Ike's possessions over here."

The mention of Ike turned Luka solemn. "Thank you."

Alannah first walked to the hotel to pay the tab and give the clerk instructions on where to send their belongings. As she walked toward Mrs. Blake's home, she dawdled, dreading the thought of talking to the old widow.

Mrs. Blake came to the door with her usual dour expression. She eyed Alannah suspiciously. "Alannah, what brings you here?" she asked.

"Mrs. Blake, I'm sure you are well aware of all that has gone on recently. I just wanted to make you aware that Luka Gunther will be recovering in my home now that he can leave Dr. Hardy's office."

"Absolutely not. I made it very clear to you that there would be no consorting with men in a home that I own."

"I can assure you there will be no consorting as you like to say. Luka can barely walk, let alone consort. I've saved myself all these years and I'm not about to change at this point in my life. He is going to stay in my home whether you like it or not."

The old woman let out a huff. "And I'll have Marshal Kelly throw you out of my house is what I'll do."

"I'm not sure if you are aware or not, but Father Mulder just went to the jail and put an end to Marshal Kelly threatening to charge me with murder for saving Luka's life. That's how pleased the Father is that I helped Luka."

"So Father Mulder approves of you letting Luka convalesce in your home?"

"He said that the town should throw me a parade for all that I'm doing for Luka," Alannah said to avoid directly answering the question.

Mrs. Blake huffed again. "Well, if it is all right with Father Mulder, then I surely have no call to disagree. Just make sure he doesn't overstay his recovery."

"Thank you, Mrs. Blake." Alannah turned and skipped away before the old woman had time to change her mind.

When Alannah got back to her home, she found Luka still sitting on the sofa. His eyes looked as if he had been crying and had hastily wiped away the tears when he heard her coming.

"What's wrong?" Alannah asked as she sat down next to Luka.

Luka grinned in embarrassment that he'd been caught. "Sometimes when I'm alone, I get to thinking about Ike and Irene and the kids. I miss them all so much and I feel so guilty that I lived and they didn't. They had so much more to live for than me, but here I am, the only one left."

Alannah patted Luka's leg. "I understand completely. You should grieve for them all that you need to, but there is no reason to feel guilty. You didn't do anything to cause all that has happened. Sometimes things just turn out the way they do without us ever understanding the why of it. We just have to make the most of the lives we have left. I know that's what I'll be doing with mine from here on out. We'll always remember them and honor them, and I hope they'll look down on us and be proud. Irene never took sides in our affairs, but she hated that we never got married. I know she would be thrilled for us."

Luka wiped his eyes with his sleeve. "Life is sure going to be different without Ike bossing me around all the time."

"You have me for that now," Alannah teased.

Smiling, Luka said, "We have one more thing that we need to discuss that we've avoided. Where are we going to live?"

Alannah took Luka's hand. "I wondered when that subject would come up. Luka, I've already decided that I will live wherever you want to live. I promised God that if you lived I would go anywhere with you and I meant it."

"I really do appreciate that, but you've never been away from your family and you may hate Bozeman. It's not much of a town."

"That's all true, but I may love it, too. Nevada City isn't much of a town either. If you want to stay up there, I thought that I could run the trading post and you could run the ranch. I certainly could manage a store with my eyes closed."

Luka nodded his head, but he was already lost in thought. "Here is what I think we should do since you are so open-minded – we could move into the ranch house back in Bozeman and stay there while you get to know the town. We'd wait on rebuilding the trading post. And if you are happy, we'd make us a life there, and if you are not, we'd come back here. I have a lot of mixed emotions about this town. I always have and I always will, but I want you to be happy. I'm not sure what I would do for a living. Maybe Marshal Tompkins would keep me on as a deputy marshal. What do you think?"

Alannah grinned and leaned over to kiss Luka on the cheek. "I think we've finally learned the art of compromise. I do love you."

Chapter 29

Nevada City, Colorado

In the month that followed after Luka got shot, he made a slow but steady recovery from his wounds. At first, he could barely take ten steps without getting winded and racked with pain, but he persisted with his walks until he'd regained his stamina. The only time he now experienced discomfort was when he coughed or sneezed. Dr. Hardy had warned him that the condition might last a lifetime, but Luka considered it a small price to pay compared to Ike losing his life. By the month's end, Luka finally felt like his old self again even if he still experienced a bout of the blues on most days. He missed Ike terribly. The two had spent so much of their lives together that Luka sometimes felt as if he'd lost a limb with Ike's passing.

Nevada City had finally returned to normal after all the rumors and gossiping had run their course. Marshal Kelly and Mrs. Blake had given Luka and Alannah a wide berth. Both apparently feared provoking the wrath of Father Mulder if they interfered in the couple's lives.

Luka and Alannah had adjusted well to their new living arrangement. Even though the experience was something new for both of them, they had managed to navigate the change in their lives without getting on each other's nerves for the most part. It helped that once Luka got better, Alannah had resumed working at the store, giving them time apart from each other. As Luka recovered, the sexual tension between the two of them became palpable. Each day they found it harder than the last to content themselves with petting. Alannah had almost given in one night, but a burst of conscience has caused her to slap Luka's hand away as he fondled her breast.

The arrangements for the return to Bozeman had all been made. Luka had purchased supplies, a buckboard wagon, and a team of horses to take Ike back home. He didn't want to part with Ike's favorite horse, Nate, and planned to tie the riding horses behind the wagon for the trip. Though Luka hadn't expressed any concerns to Alannah, he worried about making the journey with her. They had a long way to travel and she had never experienced life on the trail where most nights would be spent in a camp. He hoped she would be up for the adventure.

The only thing left to do was to get married and that day had finally arrived. Luka had the house to himself as he got ready. Alannah's sisters had whisked her away early that morning to get her all dolled up for the big day. The only fly in the ointment was whether her father would show up for the wedding.

After Luka put on his new suit, he went to the mirror to comb his hair. He couldn't help but to grin at himself. After so many years of frustration, Alannah O'Sullivan was finally going to be Alannah Gunther. His only regret was that Ike and Irene couldn't be there with them to share in their happiness. With one final rake of the comb through his hair, Luka went outside and climbed into the buggy that Dr. Hardy had loaned them for the day.

Judge Carmichael had agreed to marry the couple at the city hall. He and Luka had been friendly with each other since the days of Luka being a deputy in Nevada

City. Luka walked into the hall and saw the judge along with Alannah's brothers and brothers-in-law. Connor O'Sullivan was nowhere in sight.

"Where is everybody?" Luka asked.

Alannah's brother, Charles, turned toward Luka. "All the women and children are in the side room over there. Dad isn't coming. We all tried to reason with him, but you know how he is. I'm sorry, Luka," he said.

Luka nodded his head. "I didn't really think he would anyway. I'm just sorry for Alannah's sake. I know what it would have meant to her."

The conversation ended with the commotion of all of the women and children except for Alannah filing into the room. Luka did a double take when he spotted Wanda and Betty Anne amongst all of the O'Sullivan women.

Nora walked over to the men. "Charles, go out the front. Alannah is walking around the side of the building right now. You're the oldest and will have to be the one to walk your sister down the aisle."

Charles nodded his head and walked out of the building.

"All right, everyone, let's take our seats. Luka, you stand up here by me," Judge Carmichael announced.

As the crowd was getting situated, Charles walked back into the room. He grinned and arched his eyebrows before taking his seat with the family.

A moment later, Alannah entered the city hall on the arm of her father. She wore the same lace white dress that all her sisters had been married in. While everyone stood, Nora began crying at the sight of her daughter and husband walking down the aisle.

Luka stood there stunned by Alannah's beauty. He'd never seen her prettier than at that moment. His attempt to remain solemn failed, and he grinned like a kid at the candy counter. Alannah smiled back at him.

When Alannah and Connor reached the front of the hall, the judge asked, "Who gives this woman to be married to this man?"

"I do," Connor answered in a surprisingly loud voice.

After Connor took his seat, Judge Carmichael said, "Thank you all for coming today to this blessed event. I've known both Luka and Alannah a long time. While I know Luka much better than Alannah, I've been around her enough to know that she is a wonderful person. We're all aware of what a kind and thoughtful woman she is. I've never heard a bad word spoken about her. And what Alannah did about a month ago is one of the bravest acts I've ever known anyone to do for another. We all wouldn't be in this city hall today if she hadn't followed her instincts. As for Luka, I can honestly say that he is one of the bravest and most honorable men I have ever known. In all the years that I've known him, I've never witnessed him do anything but the right thing. I can't think of a couple that is a more perfect match for each other. The fact that this love of theirs has survived all these years to finally come to fruition today is a testament to an undying commitment to each other. All right, that's enough talking by me. Let's get this wedding going. These two have waited a long time for this." The judge launched into the ceremony. "I now pronounce you husband and wife. Luka, give that bride of yours a kiss to seal the deal."

As Luka kissed Alannah, the family stood and clapped.

"Ladies and gentlemen, I'd like to introduce you to Mr. and Mrs. Gunther," Judge Carmichael proclaimed.

The family and saloon girls descended on Luka and Alannah with hugs, kisses, and handshakes.

Just before the couple was set to leave, Connor pulled Luka to the side. He held out his hand, and as the men shook hands, Connor said, "Luka, welcome to the family. Today, for the good of everyone, I gave up on something that was very important to me. I've come to realize that Alannah's happiness is more important than my wishes. I only hope that for the good of us all you can let go of all the animosity that has existed between us for years. I'd like for all of us to start with a clean slate toward each other."

Luka smiled. "Yes, I can do that. You've made Alannah very happy today, and her happiness is the most important thing in the world to me – I promise you that."

Connor still had a grip on Luka's hand. "Good. Maybe you can at least give me a bunch of Catholic babies. That seems like a fair compromise." He winked at Luka.

"Sir, if I don't, I can promise you that it won't be for lack of trying," Luka said and gave his own wink.

Luka returned to Alannah and the couple walked out of the city hall with the crowd following them out the building. He helped Alannah into the carriage, and with everyone waving goodbye, the couple headed for their home.

When the newlyweds reached the house, Luka escorted Alannah to the front door and swooped her up off her feet. She let out a squeal and a giggle.

"Mrs. Gunther, I've waited more years than I care to recall for this day. I hope you're well rested because I plan on loving on you through the night. I have a lot of time to make up for."

Alannah let out another giggle. "Mr. Gunther, actions speak louder than words so I hope you are a man of your word. You aren't the only one that has waited forever and a day for this moment. Take me through that door. I have literally waited a lifetime to wear this dress and now I'm more than ready to shed it."

About the Author

Duane Boehm is a musician, songwriter, and author. He lives on a mini-farm with his wife and an assortment of dogs. Having written short stories throughout his lifetime, he shared them with friends and with their encouragement began his journey as a novelist. Please feel free to email him at duaneboehm@yahoo.com or like his Facebook Page www.facebook.com/DuaneBoehmAuthor.

Made in the USA
Coppell, TX
13 April 2020